The High Road

The High Road

EDNA O'BRIEN

Weidenfeld and Nicolson
LONDON

First published in 1988 by
George Weidenfeld & Nicolson Limited
91 Clapham High Street, London SW4 7TA

British Library Cataloguing in Publication Data
O'Brien, Edna, *1936–*
    The high road.
    I. Title
    823'.914 [F]

ISBN 0-297-79493-0

Printed in Great Britain by Butler & Tanner Ltd,
Frome and London

To my grandson
Jack Redmond Gébler

God that berreth the crone of thornes
Distru the prud of womens hornes . . .

CURSE

Mother mother I am coming
Home to Jesus
And to Thee . . .

HYMN

One

It rose, swelled, then burst and dispersed in a great clatter of sound. First it seemed to be a roar inside my head, a remembered roar, a remembered summons, but then through the warrens of sleep it became clear that it was a roar being uttered at that very moment, either in the room or on the landing outside. I thought I heard my name – Anna, Anna – being uttered with malice.

My hand went instinctively towards the bedside table only to find that there was no lamp, nor table where a lamp could be and then slowly and unnervingly it came to me that I was not at home, that I had come to this place, this new place, and gradually I remembered my walk of the evening before, the strange town, a mountain and now this intemperate roar while it was still dark. I prayed for it to be at least getting on towards morning, morning that would bring little respites such as bread and tea, morning that sent all crawling things and madmen back to their lairs. It was Easter Sunday, I remembered that.

I reached to the other side of the bed where I knew the lamp to be, but as I clicked on the slack button no light came. I clicked and clicked thinking at first that it was the faulty button but soon it dawned on me that there must have been a power cut. The maid who gave me the key had predicted that, and rats. She had taken me into a shed, pointed to a dark corner behind some wood shavings and bricks and with her fingers to my throat, demonstrated an attack. She had also pointed to where she lived, a few houses away, beyond the bridge, and had said through elaborate gestures that if I was in peril I was to call her. 'Celestina, Celestina.' She shouted her own name and laughed at her bravura.

I felt for the torch and in the wan light I staggered to the window to call 'Celestina, Celestina.' Parting the shutters a fraction I saw that outside, sitting on the low wall of the bridge, was a man in his shirt sleeves, paring his nails with a carving knife and still shouting. The shout I learnt to be a series of 'Nah' that he strung together as he lashed out at life. I did not go on to the balcony but stood between the barely opened shutters, thinking that by standing there I would induce him to go away. I spoke or pretended to speak to an imaginary person in the room, the one I wished was there. He glanced up. He was without coat or jacket and had a scowl on his face. It was a thin face, like the picture of a gaunt mariner on a cigarette packet from long ago, and his hair was a fuzzy white like bog cotton. My reasoning was that he would not break into the house once he saw that I was on guard. In time he got up and sauntered off, waving the knife as if it was a little skittle.

The insect-like hands on the black digital clock told me the worst, that it was only five; hours before the shops opened, and that maybe being Easter Sunday, they might not open at all. In them somehow rested my refuge. I imagined cowering there all day, allowing time to pass and knew now that I was sadly mistaken in coming. I opened one flap of the brown shutter, the better to see my room. There was a bed with a carved headboard, a kitchen chair, a horseshoe on the whitewashed wall and a photograph of a girl in a leotard, sitting on a bed, apprehensive before she stood up. Somewhere in her limbs and the recesses of her frightened being she was trying to find the pluck and resolution to get up and dance, to bedazzle an unseen audience.

I recalled the rest of the house as I had seen it when I arrived late the previous evening and had in desperation gone to the hotel to find a room, only to be turned away. There was the big entrance hall which was a wilderness of rubble and cement, a kitchen with a stone trough for a sink, on the draining board a colony of ants thick and countless as pepper, crawling ceaselessly over an orange rind. In the adjoining room the remains of a fire, as three logs staggered over a pit of cold ashes, like three faltering witches. I threw the few belongings that I had unpacked into one of the canvas bags, turned the horseshoe the way it should be, for luck, dragged the bags down the stone stairs and over the rubble, unlocked the front door, then from the outside locked it again, and put the big warped key in a crevice under a large stone, where Celestina could find it. I was going home.

I waited until it got light and then set out with two of the heavy bags, meaning to bring them a little way, then return for the next two.

> 'The wren, the wren, the king of all birds
> St Stephens day was caught in the furze
> Although he is little, his family's great
> I pray you good landlady give us a trate'

I heard the verse before I saw the speaker and for an instant I thought it must be the madman.

A sandy-haired man emerged from a path, doubling over with laughter, his bright hair like a vivid crest in the early light. He was tall and gangly and obviously amused by the sight of me carrying one bag, putting it down then running back to get the next one, talking to myself, pacifying myself, abjuring myself.

'Top o' the morning to you,' he said in a pronounced brogue and asked if by any chance he could be of some slight assistance. He waved a sailor's cap, doffed it, and came towards me, introducing himself as David Anthony Ignatius Donne, better known as D'Arcy. He had hard blue eyes, sharp features and he wore a navy smock which was spattered with various coloured paints. Between his teeth he held an amber cigarette holder and was as he said in dire need of a weed. As I went to get the next bag, he followed and jauntily hoisted it over his shoulder, then realizing that there were books in it, he said he hoped I was not a word-pedlar, who had come to drink deep from the Pierian spring.

'I can't stay in there ... it's a builder's yard,' I said, quite disgruntled.

'Has Salome worsted you,' he said with a twinkle, though he saw no reason for such agitation. Where was my cosmic consciousness!

'I'm going home,' I said.

'Ah, a Bethlehemite,' he lamented, then went on to laud the providential fact that like himself I was a descendant of the trilobed-foliaged, leprechauned folk, hence on the run from myriad forms of knackers and massacrers.

'Too many swine ... did not Geraldus Cambriensis find a similar odiousness in the twelfth century ... never seen so many swine as in Ire-land, anger-land ... have you thought of that ... that little association,' he said with a sort of glee.

'Is there a taxi in the town?' I asked, a bit curtly.

''Tis like this ... there is and there isn't, he works when he wants to ... he's newly married ... poor bugger.'

We began to walk together along the dusty road with him spouting snatches of history – 'the first conquest by King Jaime of Aragon in 1229; peasant revolt in fifteenth century, great dexterity in slinging; Archduke Luis Salvator responsible for many magnificent palaces, lover of one Catalina Homan, whom he kept imprisoned on a rocky headland, guarded day and night by wolf-hounds; another Catalina stigmatist and saint ... mark the name,' he said with casual clairvoyance. 'Catalina ... the Beata whom Satan tempts with sugar.'

From behind we heard someone running, and turning I saw that the madman was trying to catch up with us. Having cadged a cigarette from him D'Arcy pointed to me and said, 'Deutsch, Deutsch ... Heidi ... Heidi ...' pretending I was German. The man gave me a look of such disdain, recognizing me as the woman who had disturbed his matins, his toilette, and he turned away as if repulsed.

'Pay no heed,' D'Arcy said and went on to explain that the man had been a nuclear physicist but that the chemicals had

4

got to his brain, hence forcing him to quit, and that now he
was a poet of some sort and threatened to read his verses
aloud in the village bar, once the season had started.

'Agenbite of Inwit, out of his fucking mind...' D'Arcy
said, the man still within earshot. D'Arcy paused for a minute
to light his cigarette, then fixed it daintily into the holder,
while urging me to take a mouthful of my surroundings, my
arcadia.

From the reservoir, nearby, there was a croak of frogs and
on its surface a green weed that looked to be pulsing with
life and electricity. A note on a gateway read, 'Toby, we have
been three times and have made ourselves lunch.' It was
signed 'Evangeline'.

'That's how it is,' D'Arcy said. 'We open our doors to
caliphs, murderers and mendicants ... a leftover trait from
the potentate Sheik Bohibe whom King Jaime routed ...
mixed bloods here ... great for the hedge pleasure,' and he
winked and waited, asking himself aloud if I was a full twenty
shillings to the pound or not. He took my elbow and literally
plonked me on a low wall, not simply to avoid a bit of wet
tar that had been randomly smeared on a patch of road,
but as he said to see the vista in the same sort of light as
Wordsworth himself, the poor intense pastoral monk, saw
Westminster Bridge. The village looked idyllic, blond drows-
ing houses clustered together, their tiled roofs shelving one
above the other to give the effect of a sprawling fortress. The
church, as he said, was the seat of an Iberian moon goddess
long before the fishermen – with their transubstantiation
gigs – got their clutches on the needy. Terraces dropped
from the mountain, terraces that the Moors had built, in
perfect serration, with trees and half-trees clinging to them
tenaciously.

'And they're not going away,' he said with a touch of
mischief.

Where would I go? I could not go home, of that I was
certain. I thought, in that mindless way that one does, that
I would go to a city, but I did not know which one, I would
find a room and burrow there like a Steppenwolf, eking out

the days, waiting for some kind of redemption.

'Easter morning ... Resurrexi et ad hoc tecum; sum Alleluia,' he said as he made rapid crosses in the air with his cigarette holder. Something about him frightened me, it was his mockery, his rasping energy and the fact that underneath I felt all was seething – amok. As we passed a cavity of a dried stream that was filled with rubbish and punched plastic bottles, he pointed ruefully and said, 'In its prime, in its winter prime it is a torrent – Torrente.'

As we walked on some shutters were partly opened, or dogs bestirred themselves and instead of one cock-crow there was now a chorus of them, loud, jubilant, proclaiming the day.

'Hosanna,' he said to a woman who peered out, peeved to have her privacy invaded. She was an environmentalist he said but like many of that persuasion wanted the sunset and the Milky Way all to herself. The locals and the non-locals did not really mix, they parried but when it came to the verities they were at loggerheads. He said that many strangers came for an hour and never left, the place putting its effulgent spell on them – bards, pseudo-bards, painters, potters, versifiers, all of whom could be encountered from noon onwards.

'Nowhere is moonlight so strong or night so amethyst,' he said in a declamatory voice as he listed the merits that nature had wrought – 'Capacious and well-sheltered harbours; bays, creeks; earth bulging with fruits, herbs, pulses and roots, vistas of olive and Aleppo pine and such a congruence of lunatics and love-swains as could not be found in Paris in its heyday, or Barcelona at the present time.' I realized only then that he was drunk. He was coming, he confessed, from an all-night seance, where to assist the levitation of 'yer man' he had imbibed liberally and also partaken of the hubbly bubbly, giving inlet to Rimbaud drifts, lilies, those pessaries of ecstasy and violets, the spittle of nymphs.

He winked and said that if I found a little plot of ground I could grow my own narcotic and not be in danger of breaking the law. Then he hiccuped to the serene king and the serene king's lady-wife and I could hear his tongue clacking as he supped on his inner emptiness. Feeling the several books of mine through the thin pile of the bag he said was it Bibles I had brought; had I come to proselytize and this brought him without any seeming effort to his favourite topic, the denouncement and excommunication of all wandering nerds, pen-pedlars, the squeezed-out Hemingways, who were not worthy to clean that much-misunderstood man's revolver. There was one in particular that I was to beware of, one who visited on all and sundry the dilemma, whether his magnum opus should be six hundred pages or the blockbuster thousand. He ranted as he thought on it, his hoary face filling with colour, going from red to beetroot, so that he seemed on the brink of a seizure. This sub-Hemingway, one Scottie, Jnr, hailed from the Midwest of America, and was to be found from noon every day in one of the bars, poised for innocents, particularly female innocents, springing on them, offering a cosmetically induced masculine hand – 'Jaysus he sticks the hairs on' – submitting to have a cognac with them, lamenting that he would be absent for several days, closeted with the Prodigious Muse, and that they would not see him until they saw him; which as it turned out would be that very evening, because these Lolitas had got inside his head; and he was sacrificing the cold pleasure of chiselled words for the warmth and dribbles of a well-heeled dug.

He went on to describe the other artists, many of them eunuched females who painted the sea and the mountains; excrescences, soulless replicas of nature which they then sold in the land of the Stars and Stripes, flogged them to predatory matrons who yearned for homespun, untortured banality. One in particular got his dander up, claimed the place was no longer primitive enough and was thinking of going to Nepal, to a remote place free of electricity or plumbing.

'Be warned, they'll invite you for footsie and cocoa,' he said.

'What kind of pictures do you paint?' I asked and he chuckled at the compliment. Turning to me almost with humility he assured me that he had not yet elevated the bicycle chain or horse manure to the realm of art or leading-edge art, as it was now popularly called.

'They are not yon customary batik,' he said and risked the opinion that they were essentially bold, making a break with the impressionism, post-impressionism and all cliché-ridden wank.

As he went up the last set of steps he strode ahead, both to show how hale he was and to lay claim to territorial rights by shouting at some children who had huddled on the steps where they were painting Easter eggs.

'Behold the town, in which Moorish, English, and Spanish kings: likewise dukes and archdukes held sway, dominated by the vista of the chapel, its backside to the town, its windows rayless.' Then he most chivalrously greeted a young girl who went by with an Easter cake with marzipan birds perched precariously along its edges. The sight of her induced him to recall the hackneyed poetic dream of the Spanish señorita, the Spanish mantilla, the blood fetish and most of all ... the Mirada ... the long gaze:

> 'that love ne drawe ye not to done this deed
> But lust voluptuous.'

Then he darted up a narrow street, in search of an inn, his hands raised in the air to show some sort of militancy.

It being Easter Sunday, the bells were ringing out, rapturous, repetitive; flooding the air with the message that Christ had risen ... Resurrexi et ad hoc tecum sum Alleluia ...

Little holy communicants in white veils, wearing white kid shoes, hitting each other with their bunches of white flowers, trailed up the hill to Mass; the little boys wore shorts and starched shirts and were the laughing-stock of other little boys, obviously the children of visitors, who were not going to Mass but instead were painting on sucked-out eggs. Some they had already painted and were assiduously trying to sell – views of the mountain, the sea, the church steeple, or the big black cannon that stood there like a tarred elephant, a reminder of historic days.

It was getting warmer and the sun gave to everything a lustre. D'Arcy was right. I would be mad to leave such a haven; girdled by sea and mountain, the mountain like great vastnesses, gold where the light struck in one place and rust-coloured in another. The ribbon of a jet arched over the summit, at first bright and metallic, then fuzzy and as it disappeared I thought goodbye outside world, goodbye all, I need never return, I can settle my accounts here.

I would grow to forget him, the him that I believed had broken my heart, but in my saner moments I recognized as being probably the last to partake with me at that fount of sensuality, and vertigo and earthly love. As with many a thing, we had embarked on it lightly, but it caught fire, escalated, went too far, to the marrow, rekindled hopes, sparked off desires, hurting even as it satiated, creating fresh hungers and fresh fears. Its end dribbled on, an end that consumed my middle years like a terrible wasting sickness so that I often wished to be quite old, thinking by then it would have faded completely, without a trace. At other moments I wished that it had never happened because the incision was too much. Then again I wished for vengeance, retribution, which I gave vent to only in dreams. At that moment, standing in that world of lambent light I would have given anything to have my youth back again, for a year, a month, a week, an instant. His letters I had returned. They were in dove-grey flitters, like the pieces of a shredded jigsaw, on his desk maybe, or maybe dumped by a prudent secretary into his wastepaper basket. I would forget him a little each day and of course in forgetting him, kill that part of myself that for all its pain is the most sacred.

'Hotting up . . . little Druidess . . .' D'Arcy said as he went down the path to an art gallery with a gaudy modern poster on the half of the door that swung open.

I climbed to the top of the town and had my first glimpse of the sea, a patch of blue between two rocks. It was of such blueness that it seemed not to be water but a potion, of

magical properties, as if a flock of peacocks had been liqui-
dized and metamorphosed to create this flagrant, saturating
blueness. Between the town and the sea were the orchards –
trees and foliage giving a softness to the landscape, a sigh,
taking the sizzle out of the air, creating a silvery stir as the
olive leaves decided to shift upwards, then droop again like
the wings of a butterfly, lazying. The air was glutted with a
smell of orange and lemon blossom, a smell that wafted
through, as if gardenias or tuberoses were being pressed
while the oranges themselves were dusk-like, mystic fruits,
globes to be worshipped, rather than fruits to be eaten.

'They come and grab you, don't they,' a woman said,
startling me. She was a blonde chirpy woman, one whom
D'Arcy had sent to regale me. She would have a place for
me in a few weeks, an apartment, above her own. It was one
of the few houses with a front gate and a child's new bicycle
lay flat on the path leading down to it, its gentian paint
flashing in the sun. She had come to the place over ten years
ago and never regretted it. Her name was Wanda, she said,
adding that it was not her real name but one she had given
herself when she moved here. I felt that like me she had come
as mendicant, a mendicant from love, from disappointment.
Her little boy Sam followed with a litter of puppies in his
arms and brought them for me to see. They had been born
at five that morning and he had delivered them. They were
utterly still, adhered together like black and white fur-backed
gloves in a shop window; silent save for the occasional little
mewl that escaped from the thick of the fur.

'We're going to sell them tomorrow, at the market,' Wanda
said, at which Sam whinged and said, 'Not all of them, only
one or two.'

'We'll see,' Wanda said.

'Oh please,' he begged and promised he would look after
them and clean up their messes and their dribbles. I knew
that he would have his way, he was her idol, blond, round-
faced, with the beauty of a child and the perkiness of a little
man.

'Please, Wanda,' he said. Saying her name clinched it,

because he said it like a lover and like a lover she smiled back, a shy yet coaxing smile, and I had a stab of memory of my own children now grown into manhood, for whom I always wanted to seem happy, even carefree, as if sadness was a disgrace, a sort of blight on one. I remembered a girl telling my son, as they thrashed their way up a public swimming pool in London, that I was not happy, and upon being told this by her, I felt mortified, and later said to my son that she had been mistaken – quite mistaken, and unable to look at me, unable to bear the lie that he knew I was telling him, he stared into a low vase of anemones and asked if they were violets and if they smelt.

'You'll be very happy here,' the woman said and added, 'You could make a life here if you wanted.' The word terrified me. A life! It sounded such a vast thing, interminable.

I had been thinking of days, or months, or maybe half a year, lurching along with my books and my memories trying to make a fist of things. She said that if ever I wanted coffee or cookies or a chat I could sneak in, as she kept her front door open.

I retraced my steps and through the window of the art gallery I could see a woman on the phone and soon after D'Arcy came out repeating the 'Resurrexi' refrain, saying I was fixed up for two weeks, at least.

'There is a woman in there now ... she's a Yank ... she'll tell you what you have to do and what you have to pay ...' he said as he summoned some of the children to help me with my bags. He would escort me himself but that he had to catch the bus as he was celebrating the feast in the city with a Dutchman, who owned a nightclub. He said in due course we could meet, either in his town house or up in the hills where he repaired to commune with nature.

The woman in the gallery greeted me without too much flourish. She was American and as she said used to being a shoulder to cry on. All sorts of people got stranded, had their money stolen, broke up with their boyfriends, or else fell desperately in love but always came to her mainly because her gallery was open and because she had a telephone. Along the walls were huge pictures, bold vistas of sea and crag, larded with purple paint that seemed about to crack.

The house she had found me was a little out of the way, up in the hills in fact, like a Red Riding Hood house, but it meant that I would have peace and quiet. I was sharing it with an English lady, who was a sort of caretaker but she was out most of the day as she cleaned other houses and gardens so I would have no one to interrupt me. As she described it I felt a pang. I would have preferred to be in the town, close to the bakery with its bread smells, close to the church with its bells, meeting the children in the morning on their way to school, then on their way back from lunch, seeing the lorries coming with the big punnets of fruits and vegetables, standing next to the people in the shops, being part of things, without knowing what they said. She explained to me that the key was in the potting shed, hanging on a nail inside the door, and that the children would escort me. The name of my house was 'Ca'an Pintada' – 'the Painted House.'

She selected three of them to be my guides, ignoring the beseech of all the others. They ran to retrieve my luggage while I myself picked up my shawl from the roadside. It looked gaudy, assertive, its threads brightened by the sun, each blue, red and yellow thread distinct from its neighbour.

'Ca'an Pintada ... Ca'an Pintada.'

The word went around the street. People who did not know me or even know of me waved and Wanda ran after me with a torch.

'You'll need this,' she said, 'you'll need this at night.' It was a flat torch and the paint had peeled.

Thanking her I flicked it on and off for some kind of security. I hated to be leaving the town and as we took to the overgrown path I hated it more. The ground was slithery with pines and there was a smell of scrub and rosemary. As we skeetered along the children laughed incessantly, bumped into each other and dropped the bags. There were steps but these were so overgrown with fern and wild asparagus that path and step had merged and at times it was a question of groping through the undergrowth. As we went down into a

valley the vegetation was higher and the children disappeared
in it. There were paths leading off from our path, some to
other secluded houses, some doubling back and connecting
with paths that led to the village and some to still higher
terraces that then seemed to straddle their way to meet the
road on the opposite side, over which cars already glided and
glittered.

The house was surrounded by tall trees, mostly eucalyptus,
and the garden was a riot of flowers. Nasturtiums scattered
over one bank looked like bits of orange peel, their leaves cool,
graceful and insouciant. Further down a bed of marigolds so
golden it was as if the sun had lain in them. There were birds
and birdbaths and on the terrace itself geraniums in huge
terracotta pots. The roses had just begun to bloom, some big
as cabbages, white roses with a pink ruched edging, others
utterly white, unstained, and still others bowing over trellises
and arches, arabesques. I thought that later on I would pick
a few and put them in my room. A hose wound its way across
the terrace and down to the moat of marigolds but there was
no one in sight. I called and waited, then called again but no
answer came. The woman in the art gallery had said that the
girl I was sharing with was a very retiring girl and that I
might not meet her for days, even weeks. I sensed that there
was some difficulty but could not confirm it.

The children gloated over the big tip that I gave them and
scampered off, no doubt eager to boast to their friends, to
prove that they had made more money doing this than they
ever would painting Easter eggs. I was sad to see them go.
The place was beautiful but there was a loneliness to it
and the house itself did not have the gaiety of the garden.
Suddenly the hose was moved by an unseen hand and as it
rose and coiled and darted away it was as if a snake had
pounced. She was indeed somewhere, but chose not to
present herself.

There were two spare bedrooms, one downstairs and one
upstairs. I examined both, thinking which would be less
isolated, less gloomy. I lay on the bed, listened for a creak or
the sound of a cistern and eventually decided on the upstairs
room, opposite Charlotte's. Her door was ajar and I saw

music tapes, cardboard boxes and endless clutter.

My room was simply furnished – a bed, a dressing table, a lamp and a few hangers on a hexagonal wooden peg where I was to hang my clothes. Through the open window the trees were pendant in the sunshine, the cypresses dark and gaunt, tapering, like darning needles threaded with rough green wool, and in the flowering oak tree convolvulus wound itself around, giving the effect of teeming butterflies, with a whiteness so pure it reminded me of the little holy communicants in their lace and satin.

I hung my clothes on the three available metal hangers, bunching blouses and dresses and cardigans together, realizing that I would probably not wear most of them, that city preoccupations would desert me here, that I would wear the same old thing day after day and for my climbing would have to invest in a pair of espadrilles. The little table was so small that I could not place my books separately, end to end, but had to pile them, one on top of the other, debating as to which should be on top as if whatever title caught my eye would in itself be significant, even talismanic. In several of them I found postcards, postcards from people I had almost forgotten, and now reading these affectionate tokens I wondered why I had come, why I had not gone in search of my friends, and flung myself into their lives, their cares.

A year earlier I had gone around America, giving lectures, the same lecture in each city, the summoning up of one's land, battle-haunted, famine-haunted land; woods and glens from where many had come, creeping forth upon their hands, looking like anatomies of death, like ghosts in search of dead carrion – thereby quoting not a Gael but Spenser, the befriender of Elizabeth, the Faerie Queene. I knew even as I said these things, delivered these gleanings of history that the soul of a race cannot be transmitted any more than the soul of a person and in trying to bring this past alive, I was both adulterated and adulterating. How could they know what it was, to walk roads and byroads where nature was savage; a landscape shot at times with a beauty that was dementing, indigo, fuchsia but for the most part permeated with an emptiness redolent of the still greater emptiness, giving a sense of having been stranded, left behind by history and by the world at large, a severed limb of a land full of hurt and rage; a rage that enters and transmutes the way moss and the damp soak into the tombstones.

Afterwards there would be a party, a makeshift party, and I would drink jug-wine from a transparent plastic glass, eat a hexagon of cheese with a grape or an olive affixed to it by means of a plastic skewer and wonder if any connection at all, other than habit, and bland courtesy, existed between these people and myself or these people and themselves.

Once in one of those places, overcome by staggering isolation, I lay face down on the gauze-like pillowslip, kissed it, and looking at the crescent of lipstick I wondered if a kiss on another person's lips or cheeks left its mark for ever, its imprint, could be traced for all of time, never to be denied or refuted.

There were two beds in that room, as I remember it, two beds with wicker headboards, and on one, the one where I lay, a handprinted sign which read, 'Hard Bed'. Earlier, and before I set out to give my lecture, the woman who kept house called me into her quarters which were like a jungle, full of thick plants that looped into each other, with little canaries in cages scattered about, piping through the thick, stagnant foliage, and with tears in her eyes she had asked me what life was like in the fast lane.

Another evening in the Midwest I went alone after my lecture, and ate in a revolving room, so that sometimes I saw a singer in a short sequinned dress, and at other times saw a bit of water, maybe a lake, then a series of arterial roads, all with cars, which because of being distant had a flicker of magic like the stars and then again I saw the one main street with the 'Black Steer' sign, but no matter how the room revolved I was listening to a young man telling a young woman that he did not think he was going to be able to say it, because he had never said it before, and what he was saying, long before he said it, was, that he loved her and wished to marry her.

I thought how the people who had come to my lecture
were going home now, along those arterial roads, in their
cars, wearing their cumbersome quilted coats and gloves,
thinking maybe or remarking on something I had said,
remarking maybe how baffling life is, how things differ
between one country and the next, the speech, the expec-
tations, the threads of hope or half-hope, and feeling probably lonely or a little bewildered as I was, as I sat in the
revolving room looking at the sign of the 'Black Steer', or
the pocket of water, eating frozen shellfish that next day
would confine me to my bed where through a window I saw
the snow swirl down so dizzyingly that I believed myself to
be inside a paperweight from which I would never emerge.
Lying there, choked with fever, or food poisoning, and
believing that I would never get out I clung to things from
my former life as if in them I could find refuge, whereas in
fact they were studded with pain. I thought of the day that
I had burned my boats with him, how I had degraded myself,
disappointed myself in both our eyes. I had cried in front of
him, cried because I could feel the oncoming chill, the way
one feels winter or indeed any season, cried in broad daylight
over thin slices of avocado and he had said, 'Maybe next time
I'll be the one that cries,' but he did not cry with me, did
not even commiserate and I saw how reduced I had become
in his eyes. Gone the days when he saw me as beautiful,
queenly, or even formidable. The time had come to throw
me off like an old garment, and yet in that snow town in
the Midwest I believed I lingered within him somewhere,
sprouting at times, being brought out into the light like a
little urchin, an urchin of his memory, and I believed it
afresh in my new room where I was intending to spend a lot
of time, to spend months maybe, to set down my thoughts,
to meet myself.

I opened one of my books at random, and read of the three
kinds of knowledge – 'the first is sensual, the second is
intellectual and is much higher in rank; the third represents
that aristocratic agent of the soul which ranks so high it
communes with God, face to face as He is. This state has

nothing in common with anything else, it is unconscious of yesterday or the day before, and of tomorrow and the day after, for in eternity there is no yesterday nor any tomorrow, but only Now, as it was a thousand years ago and as it will be a thousand years hence and as it will be after death.'

Through a sea of tears I heard a step and jumped. I reckoned it was Charlotte. She had a heavy tread, or else it was because of the bare boards of the stairs. I wondered if she was a big girl and I wondered too if she would resent me, being used to having the place to herself.

Earlier I had seen signs of her. I had gone into the kitchen, like a thief, looking at things, at this and that – bean-sprouts under a damp cloth, that looked like nipples, yet were full of beseech. In the refrigerator several cartons of yoghurt and some raw fish. The yoghurt labels had baby gooseberries hanging from a branch and the raw fish was half-wrapped in newspaper. She had laid her place for her supper and there was something a little forlorn about it and familiar – the one plate, the two pieces of cutlery, the used and refolded napkin in its bone ring; a place setting waiting for its solitary rite.

I thought to go and introduce myself but because of the crying and mulling I feared that she might find me depressing and so waited to pluck up the courage, going from the window back to the bed and then to the window again to marshal some strength. From her room there was a sound of music, pop music very loud and then suddenly as if under the sway of a command or a whim, the music stopped and I heard her dash out again. She went down the stairs at a frightful speed. I ran to the window and saw her pass beneath. I only saw her back, she was tall and had yellow-blond hair; she was wearing jeans and a red T-shirt. She could have been any age.

At about six, feeling hungry and a lot more buoyant I decided that I would dress up a bit and go to the town, maybe look into one or two of the bars that D'Arcy had mentioned.

I did not lock the door but left a little note which by its very indecision, amused me. 'Please do not lock me out,' was what it said. I did not sign it, since she must know that I was the only person living there. She had been told by the woman in the gallery, she had even been consulted, which is what the phoning was about. The woman had tried to trace her in one of the many houses where she worked and had eventually found her and it seems she had said okay, so long as we kept to ourselves and ate at different times.

The sun was going down in a great carnival splendour. Gold splashed regions of the sky while throughout were puffs of cloud, daintily fringed with pink and crimson. The smell of plants and herbs intensified, as if someone had put a match to them, as if they were smouldering, and walking amidst the bushes, over the slithery pine needles, I thought how I would make this place my home for a long time. For far too long I had hidden in cities, burrowed. I remembered a shop window that I had once seen in Boston, at harvest time, a travesty of nature, and pitiful at that. The floor was strewn with straw and there was a wire frame, in which over-white eggs were wedged, eggs covered with straw and false dung. The mannequin was modelling a greatcoat and boots but his face had been painted a sickly magenta and in his face more than in the mockeries of nature I saw Armageddon.

Two nightingales let out a range of calls that were urgent and arresting and sounded mechanical and not like notes or calls that sprung from the soft and throbbing throat of a bird. The first star appeared in the dip between two ridges of mountain and I followed it full of sudden, unaccountable optimism.

Where the path came on to the main road there was a Station of the Cross on the gabled wall of a house. That would be my landmark on my way home. It was the fourth Station – 'Jesus meets his Afflicted Mother'. Flashing on the little torch, I took a closer look at it to recognize it later. The Virgin was in pale blue, as was the other Mary who had succumbed to an orgy of tears. Both in blue togas, both supplicating. Jesus was impassive, putting a grave face on things, partly no doubt because of the stoicism of his character and partly because the painter must have kept in mind the ten more encounters, including the twelfth climactic one.

I went down the very steep hill, past the art gallery, past the closed bread shop where two remaining baguettes of white bread looked pleading and not like bread at all. Then on a whim I followed a second hill, following the Stations of the Cross which I knew would lead me in the end to the church, the seat of the Iberian moon goddess. The figures in the Stations became more and more stooped, with the imminence of the sacrifice. Through an open door a tall and sombre man was laying out a collection of shells and talking to himself. His open door meant he was ready to receive. Many doors were open and I thought as the weeks go by I will cross one of them, surely.

In the chapel grounds were the local women. They were older women with sallow faces, faces of stone; impassive, except that in the eyes there was a message which was hard, outraged and unforgiving. The years and their hardships had made them look alike, and they all wore black. Some had walking canes, while others limped and all had grey hair ridiculously rinsed with blue and were primly permed. I felt daunted, yet at the same time I followed them, as if drawn to them in a kind of surrender. They were calling me to their camp, to their way of life, to a repentance and a contriteness that I was not ready for, not yet. I stared back at them and in staring I believed that I was defying my own mother who had pervaded and begrudged every moment of my sleeping and my waking life, persisting even after death. In their eyes, as in hers, were uncharted vortexes of hurt and rage that I believed went back to their own mothers and their mothers' mothers, figures who had usurped their lives from them.

Inside, the chapel had that aura of gloom and theatricality that I could never resist, that uniting of blood and glitter. Up along the aisles were a series of altars, little altars all decked with statuary and flowers. There were statues of the Virgin, St Teresa the Carmelite, St John of the Cross and Christ with a gold-threaded apron around his loins. Mass was soon to be said. On the main altar the candles were ready to be lit and on the pulpit a little metal microphone for when the priest would give his sermon. The women had knelt close together, formed a phalanx, and begun to recite the rosary. I sat a little further back. I did not want to pray and yet I wanted to be there, in some secret recess of my being I wanted a link with them, a soft look, an exoneration maybe. As they commenced on the litany their voices blended to a uniform murmur, a sort of drone that was sub-human.

Mater purissima,	Mother most pure,
Mater castissima,	Mother most chaste,
Mater inviolata,	Mother inviolate,
Mater intemerata,	Mother undefiled,
Mater amabilis,	Mother most amiable,
Mater admirabilis . . .	Mother most admirable . . .

Above the tabernacle was one of those Virgins, or perhaps the sum of them, the Immaculata, ascending to the clouds, crushing the serpent rather demurely with her bound plastered feet. Above her was the Sacred Heart, with spikes of gold streaking out from his Heart, skewers of pain and beatitude. Two points of painted flame above him made shadows on the arch, and looked exactly like the bloodied points of two butcher's knives. Now and then one of the women would look back to see if I was still there or if I had joined in. The looks became more interrogative.

In the end I skulked out and crossed through a gateway into a graveyard, which by comparison was cheerful, glowing with life. The slab stones were flat and friendly, each one engraved with simple childlike lettering, giving the name and the lifespan of each person. On most of them there were flowers or herbs or quaint little souvenirs, things people brought from their own houses and left there – ornaments, mementoes, a hand-written poem.

It was growing dark. The sea had relinquished its blues, its greens and its violets and was now like a great, dark, recumbent wet mother; mother of creatures, animate and half-animate, mother of life and death, moon and star, mother of the unknown; indifferent to the wretched pleas or cries of man.

Two

In the restaurant that overlooked the mountain I found myself next to a lively group. They seemed like a troupe of travelling players, dressed in exotic clothes and talking rapidly in various languages. Two of them, very young girls, had their faces painted starkly white, like clowns, and their eyelids were a hooded terracotta. The younger one suddenly stood up on a chair, unfastened her very short dress which fell to form black pantaloons, with pink-lined pleats. People cheered. Her movements were very delicate like the movements of a flamingo. She put the palms of her hands forward like an Indian dancer, thanking people for admiring her brief performance. The man at the head of the table was dressed completely in black, a black silk kimono, black silk shirt and black glasses. Behind his glasses I could feel that he was looking at me, that his eyes were directed on me and I felt a little self-conscious at being alone. My table had been laid for two and there were two carnations, looking idiotic in a big ceramic vase. I ordered fish and a half bottle of wine. They only had full bottles but the waiter said he would bring the whole bottle and I could drink what I wished, then he would write my name on the label for the next time.

'You come back,' he said, and asked where my husband was. I would take a sip and look out at the mountain which was now a hulk of darkness; the sky above it riven with stars. Then I would jot something in my notebook, simply to give myself something to do. But all the time I was aware of the merry group and aware of the man's eyes, behind his glasses, fixed on me. There was something very still about him, still, like a soapstone Buddha, and it was clear that he was the centre of attention, and all were beholden to him. The young girls kept throwing things at him, bits of bread, shreds of the carnations, a feather earring, anything to get his attention. The starkness of their painted faces belied their frivolity. One of them looked down at her ice cream which was in a coconut shell, then lifted a thin crescent of dark chocolate off it and gave it to him to eat. He in turn gave it to another girl, a quieter girl next to him, who licked it from his hand. She smiled at him. It was an adoring smile, a smile that said, 'I would do anything for you ... I am yours regardless.' An Australian man was amusing them by telling them of his many lives and his many loves. He was thin and wiry with a hat pushed back on his head, and he had that weatherbeaten look of a man who has lived in the bush. His most recent love, his little Rosie, he said had died a year ago, her little heart gave out. He prayed to her morning and night. The young girls giggled at this, but he didn't mind, said his little Rosie was in there and pointed to his chest, which was matted with black hairs. He said it didn't matter whether people were dead or alive so long as they were remembered. So long as one talked to them every day, or prayed to them, because that was food and water to their little souls. Then he told them how in past lives he had been a warrior, a woman, a gigolo, and a black hunter. He had been speared in his belly, in Central Africa.

'Rubbish,' one of the young girls said. To prove it he pulled up his shirt to show a great gash on his bronzed stomach, a long gash with little gashes running out from it, like the vertebrae of a fish. One of the young girls pulled his shirt down and said there was a lady looking, referring to me. The man in black asked if I would like to join them. He introduced everybody very formally, the girls were models, many of the party were from a magazine, in Cologne, the Australian was their make-up artist, and he took the photographs. He poured me some wine, said to forget about my own bottle, to drink theirs, to celebrate with them.

The two models and the Australian then started a contest, arguing who knew the most songs from popular musicals. Soon they were singing the hit songs from *Oklahoma, West Side Story, Porgy and Bess, Brigadoon*. Each side only sang the first line in order to be able to jump ahead, and presently the models cheated by singing only the first few bars and immediately going on to another song. They became so excited that they went too fast and we could not even hear what they were singing. The girlfriend of the photographer, whose name was Birgitta, smiled at me from time to time as if to reassure me, as if to say, 'You can admire him, you can flirt with him, it's all right.' It was only afterwards I realized she was deaf and when he wanted her to know something he spoke to her very clearly and with his face close to hers. Then she would smile, as if he had told her something very special; something that only he and she shared. I felt happy with them, I felt weirdly linked to them and had the daft wish to ask if I could go home with them, to Cologne.

Later the photographer suggested that we all go back to the hotel for champagne. He took out all his money and said it was really no use to him, he yearned to spend it. It was to the hotel on the hill, where I had gone that first night, that we all trooped. There was something very heartening and magical about approaching it, it felt like a homecoming, walking up there with a group of people, talking, singing, nonchalant. The Australian ran on ahead to get us the best chairs in the main salon.

'Just you wait, 'Enry 'Iggins,' he said, thumping one of the models as he ran.

We sat on a very long sofa like people in a church and the photographer sat opposite us in a high-backed chair looking at us benignly. He was very still, yet curious, looking at each of us in turn, to make sure we were happy. His girlfriend asked me if I thought his glasses made him look sinister.

'No,' I said.

'Oh, tell him they do,' she said. 'He'll ruin his eyes, his beautiful eyes.'

'His beautiful eyes,' he said, mimicking her. But he was not making fun of her. Something tender and playful flowed between them. Suddenly Birgitta jumped up and ran towards one of their suites which as it happened led off the salon. Another bottle of champagne was brought and I had this nice feeling of being carried along, weightless, thoughtless, like a streamer. Birgitta returned with a T-shirt, a white T-shirt which had one of his photographs on the front. It was black and white, lovers lost in a forest. The woman was taller than the man, wide-shouldered and smouldering, and the man was kissing the nape of her neck, deeply, as if he was drinking from it, drinking life itself from it.

'Put it on,' she said, 'it will suit you.' I felt shy about taking off my own blouse but the Australian made them all cover their eyes until I had donned the T-shirt and they all clapped. He then ran down to the suite and came back with a fawn attaché case, which when he opened it had little tiers full of bottles with enamel foundation and little round boxes of eyeshadows and rouge. He started to paint my face; quickly, assuredly and even as he was doing it I thought, I shall be someone else, I shall escape being me for this night at least. The girls oohed and aahed and the fashion editor said what a transformation, what metamorphosis.

'Just you wait, 'Enry 'Iggins,' the Australian said as he ogled the photographer to take some snaps of me.

Soon the room was a blaze of strong lights and I was sitting sideways on a straight chair as the photographer clicked away and the girls kept making faces because they wanted me to laugh. They were setting fire to the flimsy papers that were around the macaroons and watching their ascent to the ceiling. A few people came and looked but soon got bored and drifted off again. The photographer told me that I need not smile, said he wanted me to look sad and all I had to do was think of those dirges of my native land. Afterwards he wrote down my name and address and said that he would send me a set of photographs but that it would not be until November.

'November,' I thought with a shudder, a future time that I could not envisage, did not want to. It frightened me.

After the arc lights were quenched, he put his two cameras into a clean, yellow chamois and he came and sat next to me. The magazine owner, a very tall, patrician woman, and her young girlfriend, who had not spoken a word, decided to retire as they were leaving at six in the morning. They gave me their cards and said that if ever I was in their city I was to look them up. One of the young assistants began to carry out boxes and suitcases from the suite. The open suitcases were full of furs, heralds of raw winter. There were red furs, fox furs, some silver, some blue, and still other furs so sleek and dark they brought to mind an army of morning moles crawling over a frosted lawn. The models jumped up and in their own tongue, sang a hymn, just like children, before they kissed everyone goodnight. The Australian said it would be 'pissing up a rope' to have a beer but that he would anyhow. I knew that I should get up and go home but something stopped me. It wasn't simply the journey back to my house, which indeed daunted me, it was an unvoiced notion that if I stayed with them, among them, I need never go home. The group was thinning. The Australian chuckled as he filled his breakfast order – cereal, orange juice, two boiled eggs, croissants and pastries; all to be served at five thirty. He carried his beer with him, gave me a friendly pat and said, 'See you, mate.'

The photographer, Birgitta and myself were the last. She looked at us both, tenderly, mischievously. Then she rose, kissed me goodnight, took my hand and placed it in his:

'Be good to her,' she said. 'Be good to her,' and she kissed him sweetly and left. He suggested that we sit in the little salon, where they had the fire.

'Are you sure?' I said.

'I hardly ever sleep,' he said.

'Why not?'

'I don't need to, perhaps ... I am always half asleep,' he said as he crossed to the bar and asked the young man to fetch us a bottle of amaretto and two glasses. In the morning, he said, he would tell the cashier how much we had drunk.

The fire still smouldered, and after he had put down the tray, the young barman went and fetched a great long log covered with moss. He did not recognize me as the person who had come in search of a room, Easter Saturday, and had sat in the imposing dining room, long before the other guests, devouring breadsticks and olives. Had I looked in a mirror I would probably not have recognized myself either.

'Who is this man, who is in hiding?' the photographer asked eventually.

'Oh, someone,' I said, trying to sound indifferent.

'Is he dead?'

'No.'

'Then it's all right . . . if he's not dead he's in the world . . . and if he's in the world he's thinking of you.'

'He's asleep,' I said. 'He's in England asleep.'

'Then he's dreaming of you,' he said, quietly, as if it was something he knew, something he was in no doubt of.

'Will your girlfriend be anxious?' I asked.

'It's all right,' he said . . . 'Everything is all right.' Birgitta loved him, she trusted him. It did not mean he could not love someone else, for an instant, for a fleeting night.

'When I saw you come into the restaurant I wanted to embrace you . . . you kept pulling your blouse up as if you were afraid of being seen . . . or as if you were naked.'

'I felt awkward,' I said.

'That's nice,' he said . . . 'that's very nice.'

We would not make love, we would sit and watch over one another like sages.

'I would like to make love to you but it is not necessary,' he said.

'I know,' I said.

'You don't know,' he said. 'You think you know . . . you still think it is the most important thing in the world . . . believe me it isn't . . . fucking is very overrated and coming is very overrated too.'

Then he rose and he kissed me, it was a deep kiss and there was something infinitely reassuring about it. At once I felt I

26

had exorcised the forlorn kiss on the pillow.

We sat quite still. The fire made little stirs from time to time. On either wall there were two huge paintings, that, as he said, depicted the two aspects of us all, the angelic and the murderous. One showed the backs of women in white djellabas, seated, impassive, gazing out to sea, the other was of a predator, a pig, leaping the abyss, its claws a bright bloodied pink; the crags from which it leaped were a glistening ice-green, jewelled, the same colour as those skies under which Pieter Brueghel appointed his hounds and his lonely huntsmen. We touched without touching. The touch that we almost made, hovered, was outside our hands, outside our limbs, with the antennae of our minds we held one another and I thought that this would be enough forever, this moment of pure life, this stream of abstract love.

Three

Next morning I encountered Charlotte. To my surprise she had not gone out. She was in the kitchen on the rocking chair, that had a little sway to it, a narrow chair with latticed back and a faded print cover. She was staring through the open window and I felt that her sitting there was to do with staking her claim. She had obviously eaten, because the remains of things, a yoghurt carton and the grey skin of the fish, remained on the plate. As I entered she turned and gave a sort of smile, but it was not a real smile, more a grimace and I thought I saw her flinch involuntarily. I assumed it was due to my staying out most of the night. She had a long face, with pale parchment skin and the vestiges of someone who had once been beautiful. Her face looked far older than her body, old and disenchanted.

'I hope I didn't frighten you,' I said.

'Nothing frightens me,' she said with a slight sneer. Her accent was English but she was trying to disguise it by adding a foreign intonation. The voice or rather distorted voice triggered something off in my memory and I thought of the girl I had known years before, an English debutante, called Portia, whom I had been in awe of, who was quite a few years older than me and sophisticated, with clusters of men around her, boyfriends, ex-boyfriends, one of those exotic ones who had been to Turkey and Afghanistan long before anyone else and had brought back rugs, cushions and hangings with which she furnished her flat. She caught me looking at her in this speculative way and all of a sudden she stood up and put a cloth over the beans which were sprouting. She did it aggressively as if my seeing them was itself something of an intrusion. More out of awkwardness than need I picked some oranges from the earthenware bowl, intending to squeeze them.

'I would rather you didn't use the machines ... I depend on them,' she said, and so, holding an orange by the sprig and feeling a bit crushed, I slunk down the stairs to the bathroom quarters, thinking could this be Portia with the tantrums and the legendary waist, Portia whose every whim was reported in the gossip columns, how she had had a milk bath or went ice-skating in Vienna or had thrown the gold chairs through the window of the Ritz at her coming-out party. Could this be the girl whose decrees made a thing or a person famous or ridiculous. Of a restaurant she would say, 'Best pasta in London, nearly as good as Harry's Bar in Venice when Nino is on,' then a week later say, 'It's the pits,' and send the acolytes, who waited on her word, flocking to some other place. For a brief time it was a Chinese restaurant in Whitechapel where people went and brought their own wine. Could this be she, this faded, fidgety, reclusive creature upstairs who was obviously trying to disguise herself by wearing dark glasses, indoors, in the morning? I had lost touch with Portia after her two marriages and had heard that she had joined a commune in Wales, cutting herself off from everyone including her father. Could this be she? I thought yes and no in the same instant. Portia was not someone I knew well, but I happened to be with her on one of the most important days of her life; on the morning of her first marriage. She was so nervous, and so on heat as she paced the hall of the Registry Office, in a cream lace dress, a straw hat a shade darker than her hair and a vast bunch of violets which she sniffed nervously as if they were nose drops. She mocked the other couples who were also waiting to be married.

'Look at them ... like jellies,' she said, and wondered where they got their vulgar habit of kissing, if it was not from television. As she paced she feared, feared that Pirate, her intended, would not come. I did not know her well, but I knew her well enough to see in her eyes and in her expression the look of a hunted animal. Her real bridesmaid, Suki, could not come because she had mumps, and I had been called in at the last minute because I was Suki's lodger. I had known Portia slightly but I was never one of her 'set'. In fact, she was always condescending to me. However, that morning her worries got the better of her and in the taxi she had confided that the cards were stacked against her, his mother, his bloody mother was against it, and he was so vague and so bloodless he probably would not put up a fight. I had met him once in one of those restaurants where Portia held court and insisted on ordering for everyone. At times, he believed himself to be Rupert Brooke and at other times Ronald Firbank. His bedroom was done in red silk and he had called it Veronica, after Veronica Lake. He never went to bed, he only went to Veronica.

'Come now, Pirate ... This won't do ... this simply will not do,' she had said as she sniffed the violets distastefully.

Eventually he came, beautifully turned out, tall and tapering in a pale green suit, so pale it was like the whey of milk, and he had a mauve shirt with frilled cuffs. He had been to Westminster Cathedral in search of that nice Father Something to sprinkle a drop of holy water over him to brace him for this ghastly event. His family were Catholic, and he still believed in what they had taught him at Ampleforth. Moreover, his mother warned him that if he did marry her, his sister, the chinless Camilla, would get everything. His mother thought Portia a nymphomaniac and called her Miss Slut. He did not kiss Portia when he arrived, just asked if she had any fags. A clerk led us into another room, informing us that the Registrar would come through the door in one minute, adding tersely that we had made the proceedings fifteen minutes late and had capsized their morning's arrangements. Pirate suddenly wondered if he could ask a question. I saw Portia freeze; he was going to find a reason to cancel the wedding, a snag.

'Which door does the Registrar come through, that door or that?' he asked, pointing to two doors at either end.

'That one, sir,' the clerk said, bending a little, recognizing by the piping voice and the disdain that Pirate was of the upper crust and could make a clerk, or any menial, feel very small indeed simply by the way he asked a question. This very languor was what attracted Portia, drove her mad and she used to tell the various ruses she had used to get him to bed. When drunk she used to go further and say he was repelled, didn't like her being wet and would order her to the bathroom, to shower and dry herself.

As the married couple stepped from the municipal gloom into a cold June light they were met by a bevy of photographers and journalists. The word had got out. The legendary Miss P had finally married and would be mistress of a vast estate in Cornwall. Asked where they were going on their honeymoon, Portia said coyly, 'To Bed.' Then asked where the breakfast would be, Portia said that she never ate breakfast but that chums would drop by, in the evening, and they would all watch television and have sardine sandwiches and champagne, and that they just might, might have a little orgy. She allowed herself to be weaned of the name of the hotel and sent flocks of cameramen flurrying to the one available phone booth, to give the first part of their story while promising a torrid second.

Pirate was livid. He kept saying, 'Fuck Fuck Fuck,' knowing now that the photograph would be in the paper the following morning and that consequently his mother would either disinherit him or go off her rocker. In the taxi into which we had tumbled, Portia spoke in a chummy cockney voice to the driver, popped her head sideways so that the straw hat slid off and said, 'Can you do a bunk, Guv ... can we lose the scribblers ...' Seeing her so sweet and coaxing with her wedding hat and her wedding ring and a rabble of photographers pursuing her, the driver said to leave it to him. Tearing down the street, he turned into a narrower street, jumped a red light, went further up, then cunningly took a side road which was a back route to a railway station.

31

We went up a ramp, past postal vans and railway sleepers, then down another ramp and out into a sort of wasteland where the churned earth disgorged a yellow flowering weed, and in one corner an estate agent's sign proclaiming glories to come.

'Who in Christ's name tipped them off?' Pirate kept asking.

'I'm Mrs Rowlinson now ... the Hon,' Portia kept saying as she laughed at our ghost ride, said wasn't the landscape festive, divine, just like Jaipur.

'Oh shut up,' Pirate said and asked the driver without the least semblance of manners to give him a cigarette. He broke off the filter part roughly, lit it at that end and cursed steadily between clenched teeth.

Eventually we were dislodged at Allegra's, a friend's house, for the wedding feast. Allegra had put some sparkling wine and punnets of strawberries on a trestle table, out of doors and even without tasting a sip, Pirate said he had to see someone, wouldn't be long, and he fled leaving Portia stricken and calling him the biggest shit in the world. Everyone believed he had simply gone to get hashish from Quentin, enough to get him through the remainder of his wedding day so that he could ring his mother up and warn her of the ghastly headlines. The only little anxiety was that he would take an age, that once he and Quentin had lulled themselves into a nice giggly state, they would call on other friends, smoke more, laugh themselves through the vacuous mists and think what shit, what shit that Pirate had allowed Portia to get her clutches on him. What we never deemed was that Pirate would not come back. Having married her, he felt, insofar as he allowed any feeling to trickle up to the vague repository of his brain, that he had done what she wanted, that he had married her and that in future Portia could always say, 'Oh, that was before Pirate and I got married,' or 'That was after Pirate and I got married.' Portia was too proud to go to Quentin's, the bar in Kensington where it was sure they might be. She waited, downing goblets of the sparkling wine, refusing food and then flopping down on one of the bunk beds in the nursery, not daring to believe he had done a flit, listening through her drunken half sleep for the sound of a taxi, the creak of a gate and the arrival of a loping Pirate who when he was contrite called her Sugarpuss. When she wakened around six, the truth began to dawn on her, she started to undress, tore the wedding dress from her body, tore the rosettes of lace, tore the beautiful satin slip, and tore the cuffs so that the buttons went askew and the children knelt on the floor to pick up these treasures for their dollies. The flowers she tore as well and people walked on them and pressed them into the ground. Julian, 'the Crimper' as he was called, came rushing in with the dire bulletin that in the ladies' lavatory in the bar in Kensington, Portia's name was scrawled, followed by an insulting epithet.

'What!' she shrieked.

He demurred. He said that he did not think he could tell her, that it was too hurtful, too crude. He got her to such a pitch of curiosity that she picked up a skewer from the dresser, put it to his temple and said, 'Out with it, Snake.'

'Portia Whitehead is a lousy fuck,' he said, abruptly. At first she laughed, the hard rattled laugh of the really wounded. Then she thought to go there and with her bare hands kill Jeffrey, the creep who ran the joint, and took phone messages and was the one to give Pirate sal-volatile when Pirate passed out. In her lilac knickers, scalloped with lace, she ran towards the garden gate with Allegra running after her, pulling her back, begging her not to go.

'In the lavatory!' Portia screamed as if the venue rather than the tidings was what offended her. Allegra said that they would get nice Rosie to go there later on with a brush and some red floor stain and nice Rosie would blot it all out.

Somehow we managed to contain Portia and the evening passed as these evenings do with drink and people phoning up with conflicting rumours, and someone going for a take-away and Portia smoking cigarette after cigarette and putting the ash in the very yellow oozy noodles. At one point she became calm, sentimental, said that all she wanted from Pirate was a baby and that if he gave her a baby she would let him go. Tears welled up in her as she grabbed her satin purse and said she had to find him, that once she found

33

him everything would be all right, they would go to the Connaught, she would take her temperature all through the night so that she would know the best minute to conceive, she would get that baby, squeeze it out of him drop by drop. But even as she looked in her handbag to see if she had the thermometer and as she proceeded to borrow money she was muttering obscene and mostly incoherent libels, to console herself. She went so far as to tell everybody that he had fucked Daddy before he had fucked her. He had done it in the grotto and she had come on them, with their pants down.

Next morning, apart from beholding the photographs of radiant Portia and startled Pirate, we learnt that Pirate had done a bunk, had in fact gone to the airport straight away and had taken a plane to Amsterdam, where no doubt he joined up with friends, including the one who had trepanned himself. Pirate had fled. Portia sat in the child's swing out in the garden calling him and his mother every name under the sun, swearing how she would screw him for money, every last penny, how she would sell her story to the newspapers and expose the family who got their filthy lucre from slave labour in the West Indies. There was nothing she would not tell, both what had happened between the sheets and in the back rows of the cinemas, which was the only place he could get it up.

Within weeks Portia had re-entered the fray, back to the various haunts, making little jokes about herself and Pirate being so scatty they had gone on the spur of the moment to the Registry Office, having been on their way to market to buy flowers. The marriage had been a dare and it would have been absolutely ghastly if Pirate had not done the nice thing and hooked it. She talked in mock horror of having to meet her mother-in-law, another Pòrtia as it turned out, and spend freezing nights down in Cornwall with ghastly sherry and dinner like school dinners and those awful stone hot-water jars. People believed her. Not long after, she met Martin, a 'country bumpkin' who had come with racing friends to London. She was sitting on the bar stool stringing pearls – Daddy's guilt gift, as she said – fat creamy pearls with a few fat emeralds and occasionally holding it up for everyone to admire, as if it were a daisy chain. She liked the look of Martin, weathered, from all that hunting and hacking in Wiltshire, and she said in her sweet little girl voice, 'You can buy me a drink if you like.' He bought her champagne which she drank lots and lots of, then tottered off to the lavatory, put her nail-varnished finger down her throat and made herself sick, a thing she was adept at doing. Afterwards Martin and herself went to the tap room and later on she appeared stark naked except for the pearls and said, 'Darlings, I've just got engaged to a very very naughty man.' Soon as her divorce from Pirate came through Portia and Martin were married. It was a splendid wedding with ten little bridesmaids, orange blossom and myrtle posies, an organist from Hamburg, whom Daddy the sweetie-pie knew, and her dotty mother wandering around asking if the caterers would sell her the tablecloths and the baskets of flowers at cost price. In every paper the next day Portia was kissing Martin or about to kiss Martin and announcing to the world that she wanted to start a family straight away and she would like at least six children but possibly seven. She put all her heart into country life; she wore wellingtons and long sweaters, she rode, she farmed, she gave dinner parties, she awaited her first child, which never came.

Some few years later I heard from Allegra that Martin had been having a fling with a Polish au pair and that Portia had had her deported to Poland and that she and Martin had gone to Barbados to patch things up which they seemed to do, except that the cow got out of Poland again and Martin began to see her. During or after that time I had seen her once in Kings Road walking a hound, her hair quite askew and her stockings hanging. But by then, I was caught up in a maelstrom of my own, indecisive, berserk and about to lose the custody of my children; I had left home and according to the tenets, had abandoned them. I had been too frightened to go across and say hello, and anyhow we had lost touch.

Something about the girl Charlotte reminded me of Portia, the haughtiness, the toss of the hair, a jut to her chin, all these being relics of a much more formidable and dazzling creature.

Portia, Charlotte, or whoever she was had made her territorial rights very plain. The washbasin was full of white things put to soak and the shower trough had coloured things, with bright blue detergent sprinkled over them like beading, or the sugar coating on liquorice sweets. I felt threatened. Instead of going back up the stairs and through the kitchen to confront her I went out by the potting shed door, along the garden, then through the sitting room and up the second stairs to my bedroom. I tried locking my double doors. Though at first they seemed to lock, the doors themselves began to glide apart and it was as if an unseen hand was making the metal catch slacken and loose its spring. Slowly it opened. I would have to put suitcases to it at night, I would have to barricade myself in. I waited for her to go but instead I heard her footsteps in the garden outside and soon sprinklers of water sent gauze jets over shrub and tree as she herself knelt by a flowerbed, assiduously weeding.

The sun was shining, making dazzled mirrors on the surface of the leaves, and the birds were at their most exultant. Seeing how wholesome it all was, I thought it silly of me and decided that she was just an eccentric woman who resented a newcomer. I would make friends with her. I would pretend that nothing amiss had happened. I went down, made some tea, drank it by the open window, placed my cup and saucer a little apart from hers and then went back to my room. I could not sleep even though I had not been to bed. At times I would hear the rumble of an aeroplane and at other times the sound of the birds, not a chorus, just the occasional single note, then the whoosh of the water sprinklers as they spun around. I stared at what I had written in my journal, reading it like someone in the aftermath of anaesthetic.

Mother. When I last saw her alive she was indisposed. I was with a fancy man, young, had his own reliquae of despair, but to her he was a fancy man. A touch of the

Jesus to him, long hair, licentiously ringleting, pale face
that implies: 'You have pierced my hands and feet, you
have numbered all my bones.' She was in agony, her body
and her scalp crusted with shingles. All the ire, all the fret
and all the longing had culminated in this, this harvest of
purplish scabs. She would wait for us, myself and the
fancy man to come back from our little drives, our little
jaunts and put a good face on things and thank me profusely for the presents. I would bring things that smelt
nice, eau de Cologne or perfume sachets, or scented paper
to line the dismally cluttered drawers: ploys to take the
whiff of death away. I bought her a little cooker, a Baby
Belling. Choice name. I propped it on the bamboo table
and she sat up all the while moaning and groaning. Yes,
the nurse had been, she had been washed so they ought to
be quiet for a bit, the demons, they were like lice only of
the substance of scabs, big as threepenny bits ... have a
look at them.

She thrilled to the little gift because it would now mean
she could reach out and boil an egg saucepan to make a
cup of tea, without waiting, without having to wait for
someone to come to her, to tend to her. Unspoken eons of
wretchedness and neglect lurked in the matrix of those
words, but they were not emphasized, not then, in the
flush of gladness. What was emphasized was the joy in the
new purchase, how ingenious, how adaptable, how simple;
and look, it could be carried under the arm, like a little
infant.

'A Baby Belling,' she said and let out a range of sighs that
reached far back to her youth and earlier. What unfinished
cravings calcify in us.

'You're not going to die,' I said. I was leaving next day.
I said it two, three times and she believed it because she
had to ...

Four

Charlotte was in the kitchen at lunch-time, making one of her shakes with yoghurt, wheatgerm, orange juice and God knows what else. She was quite affable, asked if I found it too hot and if I realized that there was a portable fan in my room. We discussed the weather, the tourists and so forth. She said that I came exactly at the right time. August was the worst with people eating and littering the main street. Buoyed up somewhat by this conversation I decided to venture it.

'You're not any relation of Portia Whitehead's – are you?'

She looked at me coldly and without the slightest show of comprehension but behind her eyes I saw startle, terror which in no way I could counter.

'Whitehead,' she said as if it was the name of a prize herd or some porcelain and then she put the liquidizer on full blast so that the liquid bubbled out and the cat, perched on the windowsill, leapt across to lick it. She hit the cat roughly as if to hit me.

To undo my blunder, I said fairly casually, 'She was a debutante . . . I lost touch with her.'

'I didn't think they went in for that any more,' she said.

'Not any more,' I said.

'I simply despise that world; it's old hat,' she said and I could feel the loathing as she sawed on some brown bread that had raisins in it. I knew now that it was Portia and that

38

she knew I knew, and I determined to do everything to rid myself of the secret. The thing was to make light of it and to pretend that I was in some muddle of my own making. She kept moving things, picking them up and plonking them down, simply to give vent to her anger.

'You must think me daft to have mistaken you for someone else,' I said.

'It's this place,' she said. 'Everyone goes a bit loopy.'

Then I carried my cup of tea, and went out humming, to give the semblance of good will. I would have to leave of course but the question was whether I should leave at once, abandoning my luggage, or whether I should drag it with me. I had this fear of her, this fear that she would do some harm either to me or to my belongings. I suppose I felt she was a little mad, her isolation had driven her mad, as indeed I feared it would me, if I persisted in it.

Soon after she went out and called up to say goodbye. I leant out of the window and watched her go down the track, carrying a rush basket with very long handles, which she trailed behind her. Her hair was like egg yolk in the sun and there was a quickness to her stride. I waited until she was out of sight, and a few moments longer, then reckoning that she would be down on the road, walking past the reservoir, where the frogs croaked and the green weed pulsed, I decided to take a look.

Her room was locked but as with the lock in my own room it was slack and all I had to do was exert a bit of pressure for the double doors to sunder. The room was full of her clutter, the cardboard boxes with garments spilling out of them, grey-white stockings filled with things, an Andalusian shawl, tapes of music and a few paperback books, all with death or murder in the title.

Her bed was low and covered with a sumptuous Eastern hanging, with saffron fringing. Above there was an antique sword in a worn velvet sheath. On the low chest a man's morning hat covered a bowl and I lifted it, thinking maybe that it was more bean-sprouts, but no, there, among the combs and sundry pieces of jewellery, was the famous necklace, the fat cream and green beads that she had strung together long ago and had flaunted the night she met Martin. I could still see her naked, her waist like a belly dancer's, the pearls reaching almost to her navel. I felt my whole body turn to ice as the past in all its pain, bungle and longing flashed before me, hers, mine, everybody's. I saw our lives like spectres, or those pieces of paper that the young girls had burnt and sent whirling to the ceiling. They would all be back in Cologne now and I wished that I had braved it and gone with them. It hurt, with a raw hurt, to recall our gadfly days, and yet I did, our days, nights, beaded jackets, shawls, nightclubs where we sat till three and four in the morning and sometimes had our hands read or were given bunches of roses or heather that the gypsies sold; those days when every new love affair brought us, as we thought, to the brink of a sustained happiness. I thought of the day I too had gone a bit mad, slipped from behind this girl with all these hopes to the woman who would count in morsels from that moment onwards the pleasures and excitements of her life. I was going away with a man, a doctor. It did not matter how long I was going away for, the thing was, we were going to a secret rendezvous and at the end of it our fates and our futures would be bound together. It happened to be the day of the school fete. I had gone early and saw my children flushed and merry, entering for this race and that, and had arranged for them to be with a friend overnight. I was in my own house waiting for him, sitting down, dressed for travel, well aware of the afternoon passing, but in no way doubting and still possessed of hope as it grew dark and the shrubs outside the window became blurs and the clock chimed hours that were not daylight hours. He was a doctor; he had had an emergency call, a series of calls, a birth maybe; a home delivery; but he would come, otherwise he would have telephoned; his not telephoning meant he was coming; that was for sure.

When my children came back the next day with the au pair girl, who had also returned from her own little tryst, I noticed the strange look on their faces, the shock, as they saw me there sitting in the chair dressed to go out as I was dressed the day before.

'Is Mama sad?' one child said without quite knowing what it meant.

'Bitch ... Snake,' Portia said as she burst into the room and saw me standing there holding the necklace. She had guessed my intention. She had deceived me into thinking that she had left for the day, when in fact she had doubled back, come up by one of the more hidden terraces and crept in, unbeknownst to me.

Her eyes were so violent, the sockets seemed to be filled with blood. They were no longer the pale blue eyes of a woman, but those of a bull. As she crossed I imagined she was going to strike me. She picked up the scissors, snapped it open and then started to cut the necklace. She cut viciously, making quick, hateful jabs so that the beads with their snouts of white thread went falling all over the floor, the fat cream beads like rosebuds and the green like artificial grapes.

'Oh Portia...' I said.

'I am not Portia ... Mutt,' she said as she went on cutting, then she laughed bitterly as she thought how Daddy got his comeuppance at last, his adored boyfriend had hopped it, ripped him of his Fabergé eggs and now he was in a wheel-chair with no one, only his virago Austrian cook whom he might have to marry in order to keep her. 'Come home, Portia, come home and look after me,' was his monthly plea. It was terrible to see the bile and the poison pour out of her and equally terrible that I had unleashed it. She crossed the room then, treading on the beads, indifferent to the way they swirled in all directions.

'I won't stay,' I said.

'Do anything you like,' she said, and she went into a little inner room that adjoined the main room. She slammed the door.

I began to pick up the beads and put them back in the china bowl, all the while rehearsing something to say, something that would make amends. Through the door I could hear her being sick. I went to it and made a last plea. I said, could we talk for a few minutes and then I would go. By the way she retched and then the way she forced herself to retch, I knew that she was telling me to get out.

In my room I threw books, jumpers, shoes, everything, pell mell into the several bags. I feared that she would come and lynch me. I flung the bags out the window, where they made an ungainly thud on the terrace beneath, and then crept down the stairs, conscious of every almighty creak. As I left the cat stroked and nuzzled my leg as if saying, 'Don't go, this is a lonely enough house already,' but I left without even turning around, wielding my bags with the prodigal strength that panic produces.

Five

In the hotel on the hill I was lucky enough to encounter the waiter who had brought us the log of wood covered in moss. He smiled when he saw me, he had something for me. From behind the reception desk he took a pot of the terracotta make-up and several little soft pink buds to apply it with. They had left them for me. He laughed as if he knew some wicked secret of mine while the receptionist reeled off the prices of the rooms that were vacant. I decided on a small room which as she said was really an annex for people with small children.

'How long do you intend to stay?' she asked.

'I don't know,' I said, and she looked at me with a certain suspicion.

I shook as I entered the dark room. The shutters were closed, the light came through a narrow slit in fretful shivers. I sat on the white crochet-covered bed and opened one of my bags to take out a toilette bag which I had bought in New York. Even in the dark I could see the ridiculous garish patterns of it. Yes I did have them, a bottle of sleeping capsules that I had carried for so long, just in case. It seemed unbelievably absurd that these capsules made in some factory in Switzerland, the grains carefully poured into one half of the capsule, then sealed with the other half, had the potency to permit me to take my life. A mad thought came to me of how they refuse suicides a Christian burial and I felt disappointed that I would not be allowed in the little graveyard behind the church, which I liked so much. Many clashing thoughts came to me, including the memory of my parents who were dead and the terror that I might meet them. I saw my mother's face as she lay inside the lined coffin, smothered somewhat ridiculously by those folds of white satin, like half-beaten egg whites, an unfinished quarrel on her face, a quarrel over her own acres, with one of her own, acres she had striven for. I had felt no pity for her then, or to be precise no surge of pity, the surge that seeps and flows through one and alters one for ever more. My dead father by comparison was serene, with a rose that a nun had put in the crook between thumb and forefinger, a red rose, his waxen skin like singed rice paper, but unangry, all anger gone. Last time I saw him alive I had brought a friend, another woman. 'Don't leave me alone with him,' I begged of her, because that was what he most wanted, to be alone with me, to say something, anything – a curse, a harangue, a plea. When the time came to leave him he conveyed us through corridor after corridor of this gaunt nursing home, talking to me, trying to shut her out, and in the end, admitting to failure, he led us into a large room, a concert room where they put on the Christmas show, where he had, as he said, astonished all by singing 'Danny Boy' in tremolo and all of a sudden in the empty room he sat in the one chair that was left there by mistake, put his head in his hands, scratched his scalp, and cried out, 'I was never meant to be left in a place like this . . . I was never meant to be left in a place like this . . . like this.'

If there was an afterworld I would meet them, them and a little sister who had died before me and who I believed had left a lining of sorrow in my mother's womb which I felt to be my natural habitat. I was not afraid of her, this little sister, perhaps because I did not know her or because she was so young. The pills I laid out on the bed, and then put my hand over each one, to count and recount them. They were like a necklace in themselves, turquoise and scarlet.

Suddenly there was a knock on my door. I thought for one

startled minute that it was Portia. It was a young girl carrying
a great bowl of flowers. I saw her in the light, because as
soon as she entered she turned on the switch, so as not to
frighten me. Her hair was thick and shiny, her skin very dark
like the skin of an aubergine. She crossed the room and laid
the flowers on a little bureau and then she turned and smiled.
The flowers seemed like a tree, branching, growing, extend-
ing, to fill my mind with something other than death. They
were white flowers on green foliage, and the pistils were of
spun yellow.

'My name is Catalina,' she said.

'Catalina,' I said, as if I should know. She would be on
the landing outside if I should need her.

'On the landing,' I said, guessing her concern.

Oh yes. She had sewing to do. Visitors destroyed the linen,
especially the French, they made ribbons of the sheets. Her
English was very clear and precise.

I could not do it, not then, she had by her sudden arrival
hauled me back. In the wardrobe I found a big quilt and lay
down on the bed, pulling it around me, half thinking that I
might sleep for ever.

I dreamed of rings. An entire room covered from floor to
ceiling with them – throbbing, darting, as if they were lizards;
had pulse, had life. Each wall arrayed with gold, silver,
platinum; rings such as never existed in any jeweller's
window. There were stones too, stones from the seashore
and stones with purple seepage in them, others with the
glisten of mineral and still others vaporous, like dew. Some
were as big and as smooth as birds' eggs, speckled eggs, and
others were tiny and fiery, like sparks. I wanted to touch
them, lick them. Likewise the floor was strewn. It sagged
and rose and resagged and rerose imparting a sense of wonder
and sway, beauty and risk. In the dream I am obliged to pick
my favourite ring and though tempted by many, by such
lustre, by such gleam and gleamings, I pick a grey-green
stone with half of its colour drained, a forgotten stone such

as might be dredged from the bottom of the sea or the bowels of the earth and left to moulder and as I picked it, I thought, even within the dream, that it was a precursor of things to come.

Six

Very early next morning young boys were hosing the walls,
the several sets of steps, the flowerbeds and the big terracotta
pots that were spilling over with geraniums, bright as grena-
dine. Those on night duty loped away, with sleep in their
eyes, nodding to those who were coming on duty for the day.
Soon there was a smell of warm confectionery and coffee
from the kitchen and not long after these young boys went
up the several stone staircases with huge basket trays on
which there was coffee, croissants and a type of bun plaited
on top, and doubly tempting because of being dusted with
fine white sugar. Flower smells, pollen smells, shrub smells
and now food smells made me feel again a nameless thrill as
in childhood, a giddiness at the onset of things.

Red and white blossoms spattered the steps and up by the
pool a slight breeze was stirring the cream silk fringing of
the white umbrellas. Everything was being prepared for the
day, mattresses put on the sunbeds, piles of fawn towels laid
on a table, coffee percolating and cakes of every variety being
put into refrigerated trays. A sleepy-looking young man
squeezed oranges on a metal machine and the halves piled
one on top of the other began to resemble Halloween lanterns.
Beyond were the orange and lemon orchards, the oranges in
clusters, cleaving together, meshed; the lemons with a greater
poise, each lemon hanging separately on its stem and in the
air showers of floating blossom, like gauze. A rosemary hedge
seemed by its darkness to be resisting the sun and yet webbed
by it as if by a glistening cobweb.

The town itself was coming awake too. A shutter opening here or there, and being fastened back. The cats had already appointed themselves on the tiled roofs. I asked the sleepy-looking waiter if I needed to book a sunbed. He looked perplexed, then shrugged, then said, 'If you want I do.' I waited and after some time he walked across, picked up one of the fallen lemons and placed it on a chair, a guarantee of my reservation. It was time for breakfast and so I made my way back to the main buildings.

She was by a long refectory table arranging flowers. I recognized her as the girl who had come to my room the evening before. Her hair was plaited, a prerogative of work, perhaps; and she had placed the plait over one side of her neck, so that when she moved it bobbed like a thong. There was something untamed about her, a sort of recklessness as she hauled flowers from a barrow and threw them a distance away, on to the table, as casually as if she was flinging wet fish. She must have felt my presence because suddenly she turned round and fastened me with a look that was half courteous and half brazen. Then she recognized me and asked if I felt better. Other girls were passing through the courtyard with mops and brooms and buckets, and like her they wore turquoise tracksuits.

Suddenly her name was called from one of the balconies up above.

'Catalina ... Catalina,' a young girl said, as she leant over a balcony holding bits of raw meat that she winced at.

'Crazy people,' Catalina said and smiled as she tore up the short flight of stairs to confer with her companion.

The flowers, strewn about the table, looked as if they had landed there in some primordial storm. There were roses, red, pink, and white; sweetpeas like wet jewels, anemones with black startling centres, and flutes of lilies, pale, waxen, saintly. They all smelt of water, as obviously they had been sprinkled at the market. There was something infinitely sweet and harmless about them and I thought how could anyone not want to remain alive, in a world where such tender things exist.

On the balcony she was laughing and frightening her friend by dangling the bits of meat. Later when she came down she described the couple who occupied that suite. The man was portly. She stuck her chest out to indicate his paunch. The girl was thin and blonde and slept most of the day. The girl loved cats and at night when they went to the grand restaurants the girl brought home the strips of raw meat. They ate very grandly, lobsters which had to be specially ordered, and they drank magnums of champagne. She said it must be nice to be a visitor, but she was not bitter about it, there was an impish gaiety to her, as she described their salon which was full of saucers with bits of old meat and bits of old fish for the various stray cats. Luckily, for everyone, they had gone on a tour that day, and the maid was instructed to do a big cleaning.

I ate breakfast on the terrace. I ate ravenously, piled different types of jam on to slivers of bread, enjoyed flavours that I had long since forsaken. It was as if the jams and the honey and the sugared bread pre-empted a life I was about to start on, instead of one that was more than half over. People sat at other tables or merely stood and looked across the orchards to the town and to the church. At the table next to me there was a German couple, a man and a woman wearing identical seersucker shorts and laced leather shoes. Soon as he finished eating, the man lit a little thin cigar which he did not draw on, he just held it there, his lower lip jutting out to secure it. The woman went on eating with a steady joyless rhythm as he delivered a monologue, which I was glad not to understand.

The mountain was a soft gold, as if gold leaf had been painted over it, and the trees were silken too and like feather. Papers were brought and passed around, waiters and waitresses went back and forth, and the cats, who looked a bit like rats, scurried under the tables to be given the pickings.

Once, I saw her pass with a vase of lilies, so tall that her face was overwhelmed by it. She moved them to one side as she might a Chinese mask, and gave out of the corner of her eye a little wink which bordered upon connivance, as if she

pitied me somewhat for being among such dull folk. Her
eyes were dark like damsons. I had this trickle of happiness,
thinking to myself that I knew someone, even as slightly as
this, and that at any moment I could stop by her table and
admire the flowers. I even thought I would buy a special
little notebook to learn a few words from her, in Spanish.

The hotel guests had appointed themselves around the
pool. Some were deep in conversation, others settling and
resettling themselves, moving their chairs to get the best of
the sun, still others already lying out, prone mahogany figures
drinking in the sun's rays. A little boy with red and blue
water-wings was at the shallow end by the steps calling for
his sister who called back to him in German. His name was
Otto. No sooner had she lifted him out than he got in again
and was beseeching her to rescue him. The Germans and the
English had divided the terrain, the English commandeering
the side nearest the bar while the Germans sat at the far end
near the line of poplar trees.

My own bespoke seat with the silly little lemon was
midway and next to a verandah, so that I could pull my chair
in under the matted roof if it got too hot, or if the shade from
the umbrella was not enough. The people stretched out on
the fawn towels were oblivious of each other and of everything except the sun. I passed these nameless creatures,
identifiable only as one with beauty spots, another with a
mat of hair under the armpits, a hip that curved so gracefully
it was like the handle of a salt-spoon. On one woman's
stomach birthmarks had formed little blue veins, inroads.
Next to her, a very thin, older Englishwoman was telling a
young man, a newcomer, about an evening coat she had at
home, an evening coat with silk revers and how she should
have *brought* it, cut a dash. She was prompted to say this
because at that moment a woman in a violet coat with a
thick lace collar arrived and looked about imperiously. Two
waiters helped her with her towels and her various baskets.
From one of the baskets jutted the dun canvas backing of a
piece of needlepoint. She wore bracelets which tinkled as she
pointed in one direction, then another, unable to decide

where she would like to sit and obviously irked that so many vantage positions were already taken. The thin English-woman shrugged, and said to the young man, 'All right for some, isn't it'; and they both watched as the newcomer went down towards the far end where the Germans lazed. Meanwhile, little Otto kept his sister busy by jumping in and then having to be lifted out. The Englishwoman went on with a story to the young man about her daughter, how they did not really need another child and how let's face it, two children were enough; and how it made her sick to see how many children some couples had, but that her daughter was a good girl, stubborn mind you, but good, would listen to sense in the end and not have a third child. The daughter was obviously the woman with birthmarks, because every so often, she called to her mother, 'Oh do shut up.'

'Men! Men,' the mother said peevishly as if the young man she spoke to was a pygmy.

A little boy of nine or ten slipped by carrying a toy cruiser and trailing a dog. I could see that the dog was going to be a nuisance. He found a single bed that was not next to anyone, away from the pool, one that had obviously been left there by some absent-minded waiter when he was called away.

The fashionable woman was invisible, having withdrawn under two umbrellas, and spread her baskets and para-phernalia around her. Suddenly the calm and composure of the place was disturbed by a rude English voice.

A proud father was addressing his little boy as he lifted him up and carried him towards the pool.

'Now say one, two, three, go,' he said to the little baby who whinged and refused to say it.

'Okay, let me hear it again – one, two, three, go.'

'Daddy and baby Michael go towards the pool,' he says as he goes down the metal steps, holding the irate baby.

'Cold . . . is the water cold?' he asks loudly.

'Look at the thermometer,' a woman's voice says, sharply. It is the imperious woman under the two umbrellas and her voice sizzles with disdain and authority. People laugh. The

elderly Englishwoman laughs so much that she has to take
the cigarette from her lips to cough.

The baby screams but its father is undaunted.

'Kick, kick, kick,' the father says while the baby cries and
exclaims that the water is too cold. Little Otto deserts his
perch on the ladder and runs about with his red and blue
bands, waving his arms like a butterfly.

'The water's not cold ... Daddy doesn't feel it cold ...
warm ... warm water.'

Proud now and masterful since they are the only two
people in the pool, the father inveigles the baby to kick.

'Daddy says, baby Michael has got to kick.' Baby Michael
refuses, says he does not want to, causes such a furore that
the dog who had been sleeping or dozing quietly under the
boy's chair jumps up and starts to bark furiously. People on
all sides declare that things are getting out of hand. The
haughty woman is sitting up and in disbelief asking if she is
in Blackpool, or Benidorm.

'Take him out,' baby Michael's mother calls.

'Not yet Mummy. Baby Michael has got to do three kicks
... like this, one, two, three ... And then Mummy is going
to order him a hot chocolate.'

'Or the municipal baths in Tokyo,' exclaims the haughty
woman.

'Better bring him out darling,' the mother pleads.

'Daddy's going to bring you out and Mummy's going to
wrap you up in a towel and order you a hot chocolate,' the
father says as he hands the baby to its mother and then, not
to be intimidated, he dives into the pool, splashing furiously
and churning his way to the opposite end, much to the
irritation of people already discomfited. The German couple
whom I had seen at breakfast order their first snipe of champagne and others jolted out of their languors are asking for
tea, coffee, orange juice, Campari while the waiters move
with the utmost servility, ignoring the barbs that are being
exchanged.

The imperious woman in the violet coat is suddenly standing over me and asking me if I find it as Bolshie as she does.

She asks, she says, because when passing she could not fail to notice the book on my table. It is the final volume of *Remembrance of Things Past*. Her voice is soft and in addressing me it is as if she is helpless.

'Oh, very déclassé,' she says. Her eyelids are covered with silver shadow and her hair which is also silverish is strewn with little diamanté things which glitter like dew. A woodland creature. Although no longer young, she is extremely slender and to emphasize her slenderness or perhaps to give vent to her temper she keeps tightening a snake belt which she is wearing around her waist. She asks if I would mind terribly if she were to take the empty chair next to me. Meanwhile she flicks her finger and wags the braceleted arm to alert the waiter to the fact that she needs her baskets and her belongings moved. Then she orders a *citron pressé*, in three languages, Spanish, English and French, stressing the fact that she does not want sugar. She introduces herself formally but I only catch her first name which is Iris. As she lies back beneath the umbrella she starts to chuckle, murmuring under her breath – 'their awful bellies, their hideous bikinis, their bags with trade names plastered all over them and as for baby Michael he should be put in the deep freeze.'

'Who is that child with braces on his teeth and all that sticking plaster who is allowed to bring a mongrel in?' she asks the waiter as she taps her long pearled nails on the lid of her lacquered box. He chooses not to understand and within his hearing she calls him a *burro*, a donkey. She asks me a ream of questions about myself but never once waits or even pretends to wait for an answer to any of them. I was her new friend and she was going to give me lots of tips, the phone numbers of the best restaurants in Rome, Venice and Paris, secrets. For instance, if in Paris I wanted a late lunch, *à deux*, and felt like caviar she knew exactly where I should go. The patron, who was of course Russian, Georgian in fact, made these divine blinis and did not use grade A, or even grade B but still a delicious caviar which tasted just as good. She would write out these addresses for me and by offering to do this she hoped that I realized we were chums.

'When in Rome do as . . .' she said coquettishly and reeled off her plans for the months ahead . . . Biarritz in August . . . Milano in September . . . New York in the late fall . . . Paris when she felt absolutely homesick or wanted her hair done, although to be fair the chap in Rome was better at cutting, far better . . . a sculptor, absolute master, could make any head of hair a work of art, knew exactly how it should look. She shook her hair as if on a swivel. It was thick hair and it had been dyed a beautiful ashen silver. The little diamanté ornaments looked like petals now, that had fallen from a tree. Suddenly she was laughing, saying how nice to make a friend, that it was Proust who did it, always Proust and then to her great and astonished delight she was called to the telephone. It was the sleepy waiter who called her and at first she did not know whether it was for me or her. Realizing it was for her, she jumped up and ran like a gazelle, past the other beds, apologizing sweetly, then past the tables, to the phone, which was behind the counter. I had stood up along with her because a habit, or rush of hope had made me believe the impossible, which is, that it was for me, that the man whom I had repudiated, yet hoped for, had traced me. She had her back to us but by the movement of her shoulders I could see her excitement and I guessed that it was a beau and my disappointment sharpened all the more as I slunk in under my umbrella, to give way to a surge of tears.

Sitting there in the sun, bunched up, foetus-wise, I thought that I had thought the worst was over. The worst were the years, the eternity of years that I had solemnly waited for him, believed in his coming and then put a death to it on the day when I decided to destroy his letters, choosing to drown them, rather than burn them in my grate at home. I had gone to Hyde Park, to the Serpentine, full of false hope, as if by doing this I would exorcise him, believing that the pain would buckle into rage. They were innocuous letters, quite harmless really, but because they had come from him, each word, each grey-black letter was significant, conveying more than words could convey.

It was a wet day, the wet chestnuts in flower were like

54

tassels without any tautness or any spring. The rain may
have had something to do with it, the incessant rain and the
several canoodling couples but I broke down at the moment
of doing it. I tore the letters in small pieces and dropped
them on the water where they seemed like shreds of colour-
less confetti. They lay there, tiny scraps and not so tiny, the
innuendos and the non-innuendos, words from which I had
derived so much hope, so much doubt, so much ecstasy,
each letter a little square, like a child's tooth, handwriting
portraying the oscillations of his mind that tried to cancel
what it was saying and to affirm what it had just denied.

'A drink, maybe, Wednesday, if deliverance permits.' In
that promise or semi-promise I had read so much else, his
wish to see me, which of course he had to counter with doubt,
but I knew that he would do everything to see me because
his very doubt was his confirmation and those syllables, those
characters traced on greyish headed paper, contained, and
always would contain his essence, his secretiveness and were
the precursors of our eerie love-making. All of a sudden these
fragments were sacred and dear to me, sacred as any scroll;
were all I had of him. Why was I throwing them away, these
transfusions, these utterances, that would have to see me
through, to eternity? At least they did not sink and for that
I was thankful. They had coagulated. But the words were
washed out, or washed into one another, to lose their
meaning. The ducks converged on them, mistaking them for
crumbs but did not try to eat them.

Suddenly and as if an unseen hand was skimming them
towards me they drifted back in my direction. Something to
do with the ripples of water from the duck's wings, or the
plash of the oars from the excitable punters. I took this to be
a sign and knelt and reached in and pawed them out, giving
the ducks the idea now that perhaps they were bread, or even
crackling. I held them, the damp remains that they were,
and saw the buildings that I would forever connect with the
moment – the beige dome of Harrods, the obelisk of Big Ben,
the fawn wings of the Houses of Parliament, a glass restaurant
with peaked corners, laburnum, daisies, peonies drained of

their colour and the sight of couples whose happiness was a dagger in itself.

The awful truth was, that though I wanted to throw them away I did not sufficiently want to throw them away and retrieving them was a solace in itself. I put the wet and matted pieces back into my pocket, castigating myself, and headed homewards.

Tall, grey tower blocks in which window and concrete seemed as one, surrounded me. I headed for the Albert Memorial. No reason for this, simply to walk, to get through the next minute and the one after. The grass was high and soaking from weeks of rain and the daisies were myriad. Each daisy holding on to its little bit of ground just as I was holding on to the damp, discoloured, long-since abnegated words. June, half a year gone, half another year. I saw the people as ghosts, laughing ghosts, talking ghosts, kissing ghosts, eating ghosts, linked or not linked, sometimes halting, other times moving in the rain and shrouded in it. I thought perhaps that I would never speak to anyone again or shake their hands or that such an event would be so far hence in the unforeseeable future that I would have lost the ability to do it – the hand would wobble maybe, like a prong, certainly would have lost its swivel, its suavity. The lips too. The lips that kissed a pillowslip or pieces of blotting paper, to keep in practice, would become blubber. All of a sudden there was a downpour, sealing everyone in, in pairs, with dogs or alone, or however they happened to be, and I thought this is what it will be like on the last day, we will be caught in whatever spot we are standing in and under whatever circumstances and how dearly I wished that it was the last day, lacking as I did the gumption to go on.

There was wet plywood around the base of the Albert Hall which meant that renovation was in progress, and the cupids and angels at its perimeters were grimed in soot. I thought that by the time I came close to it and touched it, something would have changed within me, that the pain would have abated enough for me to say, 'I might go to a concert soon,' or 'I must see my friends again,' but close up to it, no such thing happened and so I thought it would happen in the next succeeding moments, in the journey from the park to the roadside, where I would press the button for the pedestrian crossing and wait and watch those lines of cars, like vicious buffaloes roar up, to beat the red light, doing everything to ignore the forlorn pedestrian; that as I crossed to the other side deliverance – his very word – would come, except that it didn't. I stood to see if Bach or Mozart was soon to be performed, thinking I might buy a ticket, that my interest in life might reburgeon with those sublime and beautiful chords, an interest that would replace this wasting passion for him. I crossed the road. I read the notice regarding future concerts and walked around the circular fort of the Albert Hall, lamenting its too-red brick, and its lumpenness, yet wanting to embrace it, to be absorbed into its vast inhuman depths; then down dozens and dozens of steps, on to another street, where I set myself the same unlikely forfeit, which was that the pain would grow less, or that even if a fraction of it stayed with me it would not, as it had done in the past, immunize me to all other relations, to all other links with life, to friendships and to such innocuous things as Christmas and midsummer and people's birthdays.

My room was in semi-darkness and yet I could see the flowers, feel them as if they were breathing. It was a fresh bunch, so beautiful, so immense that I knelt before it as at an altar. Opening the shutters, I saw they were sweetpea – airy, rampant, glorious; she had included every colour, red, deep purple, pale purple, pink, and white. They were in such profusion, it was as if they had not been plucked from their high, thin, curving stalks, but that they had grown like that, in a shoal. She had added sprigs of myrtle, its pungent smell an echo of the forest, in contrast to the soft airy smell of the flowers.

I hurried out of the room to thank her, buoyed now with some purpose. She was not to be seen. The flowers were piled one on top of the other, great breathing bunches, waiting for her, for her hands to pick them up and separate them, to take the roses and pull them gently apart, the red, and the white, and the yellow roses and to take the remainder of the sweetpea that would be bruised if it was left to lie there too long; to put the tall, chaste waxen lilies into tall, chaste jars. I stood and thought that at any moment she will appear. Then, not wanting to draw attention to myself I moved away, hiding behind some trees, resting my chin on a bit of railing, thinking that if she did come, I would not know what to say, I would revert to that childhood vertigo, that overwhelming of mind and senses, as when one saw the object of one's desire, one was lost for words, or said something stupid, something blundering, even something sarcastic. I went in search of her, up various stairways, and down others, all the while meeting her companions, in their turquoise tracksuits with their brooms and their mops and their cleaning stuffs. I saw into a large room, where one of the girls sprayed liquid polish wantonly over everything while her companions bounced up and down on the four-poster bed. It was a vast suite which overlooked the mountain and had antique furniture and tapestries on the wall.

Then I retraced my steps, thinking she had been on one staircase while I was searching another. I asked one of the maids, a very quiet girl, with a faint moustache. She answered so quickly that I did not understand what she said, and so set off on another target. The young waiter behind the bar looked as if he was being disturbed from a waking slumber. The coffee machine was hissing, the brown powder falling on to filters. Whatever he thought I asked him remained a mystery to me, because he simply said, 'If I remember to, I will.'

On the way back to reception, suddenly I saw her. She was in the laundry room with a group of her companions, putting laundry into big white bags. It was clear that she was the leader because they all looked to her, listened to her, and laughed at the joke she was telling them. As she told the story she gesticulated wildly. They stopped laughing and as she turned and looked at me I found myself mortified. I rallied

and asked her if she knew how many days it took for a letter
to reach England.

'Inglaterra,' I said, self-consciously, and the others
exploded with laughter. She reprimanded them severely,
said it was obvious that they had never travelled. She told
me that if the letter went express, it would take four or five
days but that surface mail would take weeks. She explained
that one got stamps in one bodega but posted the letter in
another, and apologized for the national erraticness which
extended to her boon companions.

Lunch was almost finished but I found myself walking
towards the poolside restaurant and sitting down. Some
newcomers had appeared but they were obviously not guests
from the way the waiter plonked the bottle of mineral water
on their table. They were eating paella, the mother and father
seizing bits of fish and shellfish, while their little daughter
spurned it and was licking from a strawberry and chocolate
ice cream cone. At times she would lick it and then put it
close to her father's lips to taunt him. He begged her to have
some of the paella. She was called Fiona and the little boy
was called Ernest. Ernest did not want paella either, being
very happy with the strawberries. He had heaped a pyramid
on to a plate and was now running his spittled finger over
each one to proclaim his rights. Fiona protested, so that he
was ordered to put some back. His lips were very thin and
his nostrils thinner. He looked like a little weasel as he bent
down over the strawberries, touching them with his features.
Mother and father addressed each other on the subject of the
paella, and then on the subject of their children. To the
proud father, Fiona was a water nymph and to the proud
mother, little Ernest had the makings of Hercules. She ate
ravenously and as she chewed, she kept her eyes closed, then
opened them, to consign the choicest bits of fish first to her
plate, and then to her eager lips.

'I don't believe it, Madeleine,' her husband said; he said
it twice.

'You don't believe what?' she asked.

Her husband expressed his extreme astonishment at the

fact that she could eat at all, considering that she had such an upset tummy, had been sick on the boat, queasy all the way in the car ride from the city, vomited twice.

'But this is good for me . . . this is bland,' she kept saying, while also telling Fiona to put that ice down. Fiona ignored her and held the cone to her father's lips, but as he was about to lick it she wrested it away.

'For goodness sake . . . you spoil her, Russell,' the wife said and ordered Fiona to eat the strawberries, for her bleeding gums.

'I don't want strawberries,' Fiona said, nettled at her mother's tactlessness.

'Then you can go without,' the mother said, and pulled the remaining strawberries to herself.

The huff that might have ruined their lunch and impaired the jollity of the vacation was suddenly and surprisingly dispersed by little Ernest. All strife was put aside, all greed ignored, as little Ernest stood up, huffed and puffed, and said, 'Daddy . . . Daddy.' Daddy was ready, they were all ready, for whatever it was that little Ernest had to say. It heralded great importance because of the way little Ernest huffed and puffed, then rallied.

'Horses like hay, so, Daddy, I think that if horses had a lot of hay, as much hay as this' – he described a width of it in the air with his outstretched arms – 'horses would never quarrel and would be very happy.' The family are united again. Russell is so overcome that he stands up and announces to the restaurant at large that his son has a great sense of justice and that the world has much to learn from him.

The waiters look at one another, puzzled, amused, disbelieving.

In the late afternoon as I dozed on my bed, half-aware of the hum of life, the random voices in the courtyard below, the maids on the landing outside, there was a knock on my door, a waiter delivering a letter on a tray. It was an invitation, hand-written on the hotel's embossed ivory card. It said:

Iris Beaugrave-Mallory-Heron

Drinks

6:30 – 7:15

Hers was the very large suite that I had seen that morning, a suite with a sweeping view of the mountains. She met me at the door, in a long blue crêpe-de-chine dress and a necklace that was of single thin threads of silver and which lay across her bare throat like catgut. The lamps were lit and there were flowers on the several tables but I was the only guest. She said she had to see me, because I had been such fun, had saved her from the Blackpool Bolshies. She was leaving the following day for her finca, there had been some mix-up about dates, but she simply had to give me a drink and she hoped I liked beer because it was simply the only thing she drank nowadays. Wine, she declared, could no longer be trusted, since it made one so liverish and she asked in a taunting voice what had happened to Montrâchet, to Meursault, even to Chablis, that little upstart, known only because the English and the Americans could get their thick tongues around it, not even good enough for a vinaigrette. Then she laughed at her own asperity and led me across to a table on which there was a silver dish with thin biscuits, cat's tongues coated in sugar.

'*Parfait*,' she said, tasting one, and derided the local olives as being shrivelled; bitter and boring as their peasants. Why she came, she simply could not understand, particularly as she had read that their bulls were second rate and their men third rate. Still she had her finca and 'a friend' was coming from South America and she envisaged a very nice time, thank you very much. Her friend was wonderful, met him by the merest chance, their luggage had got mixed up in Munich and after the initial frisson he asked her to dinner. Roman Catholic of course, and with a very tiresome Catholic wife and a little boy, but they were doing something about that and life, yes definitely life was on an uptrend. She did a little swirl and then told me where to sit and sat opposite me running her hands through the silver threads of her necklace. She said, she had thought of the most wonderful thing for us to do; to make the most of the three quarters of an hour, she had set an agenda. We would each think, but really think, of the most beautiful building we had ever seen, that we yearned to return to, preferably with a lover. In the dim and artful light of the room she looked far younger; a night creature, startled, like the bark of the pale ash tree, her blue dress so sheer it seemed to melt into her arms and into her limbs.

She smiled, anticipating my answer. She even conjectured on what it might be – the Taj Mahal maybe, or Campidoglio, or one of those wonderful skyscrapers in Park Avenue, or the Russian Hermitage, or maybe an Indonesian temple. She simply ached to know. I said that, at that moment, the place that sprang to my mind was a cemetery at San Cataldo, which although a charnel-house, had the look of a theatre with its curved, coral front and bow window like peepholes into magic.

'How interesting!' she said, but I knew that she was appalled. A charnel-house!

'How interesting – how interesting,' she said, allowing a slight flinch to appear around the eyes. Yes, she knew it, of course; so charming, so humble. It was the word humble that showed her distaste. Her favourite was a tomb which had recently been excavated in China. The First Emperor had had it made for himself, countless maidens had been sacrificed with him and masons buried alive. Inside this menagerie were terracotta warriors, bronze horses, chariots; the common soldiers in battle tunics, legs in puttees, and the high-ranking officers in fish-scale cuirasses. Gave you some idea of what China was, in all its grandeur, while Europe was still a pebble pond. China was her favourite country, she loved the scale, the scope, of course not modern China with its little ant-heaps of people, spouting slogans.

The jewelled clock on the mantelpiece tinkled a dulcet tune giving the hour and she looked towards it with a seeming haziness, but within she had registered it correctly. Time to go. Calls to be made. Then her beauty sleep which was quintessential. She kissed me profusely, saying it had been such fun, God what fun it had been, and who knows, she might even persuade me to come over to the finca. She would send her beau sailing one day so that we could have a gossipy lunch, and catch up.

Seven

In the less crowded bar, where I looked, half in hope of seeing Catalina, I heard my name called as D'Arcy assailed me with a bellicose welcome.

'Enter ... enter ... Druidess,' he said, and before I could retreat he had spun me around to introduce me to his bosom friend, Gunnar, a Swede from darkest Malmo.

D'Arcy's face was a sight, wandering patches of vivid red as if cochineal had been poured on it and he wore a white fringed dress scarf over his navy overalls, which gave him a jaunty look. Since early morning he and the Swede had been drinking and sounding, as he said, the depths of their pitiful souls. Despite the language barrier and relying often on the true Esperanto they had covered many topics ranging from the trace elements in mother's milk to 'The Descent of the Locusts'. His spirits soared as he recited gleeingly and fulsomely from that brimstone buddy Cardinal John Henry Newman (1801–90).

'Brood follows brood, with a sort of lively likeness, yet with distinct attributes, as we read in the prophets of the Old Testament, from which Bochart tells us it is possible to enumerate as many as ten kinds. It wakens into existence and activity as early as the month of March; but instances are not wanting, as in our present history, of its appearance as late as June. Even one flight comprises myriads upon myriads passing imagination, to which the drops of rain or the sands of the sea are the only fit comparison; and hence it is almost a proverbial mode of expression in the East (as may be illustrated by the sacred pages to which we just now referred), by way of describing a vast invading army, to liken it to the locusts. So dense are they, when upon the wing, that it is no exaggeration to say that they hide the sun, from which circumstance, indeed, their name in Arabic is derived. And so ubiquitous are they when they have alighted on the earth, that they simply cover or clothe its surface.'

'Cats pyjamas,' the Swede said in a drunken blur and D'Arcy insisted that he tell again the story of the geese for my benefit. With mime and patchy words the Swede described how a flock of geese broke into a granary, where corn had been put to ferment, and how they devoured the fermenting stuff, glutting themselves on it, until they fell down dead. Their distraught owners decided to pluck them with the intention of selling them, even though Christmas was months away, but no sooner had they plucked them than the creatures revived, staggered up and wobbled around the farmyard, shivering, stripped of their feathers, cackling and croaking, and in goose-pimpled ignominy had to survive until the Christmas slaughter.

'Excuse me ... my English no good,' the Swede said, apologetically.

'The best way to learn English is the mnemonic method,' D'Arcy said, and spouted spoonerisms into his bewildered sweating face. They were drinking wine and local cognac and every few minutes the Swede would laugh and then give way to a bout of tears, which as D'Arcy said was bound to befall anyone who lived in the dark for eleven months a year and was suddenly exposed to decent sunlight. The Swede owned a sawmill, employed hundreds of people but lamented his position, because he felt himself cut out to be a composer or an artist or even a ceramist.

'Tough ... tough,' D'Arcy said and muttered, 'Bullshit,' to me.

'Shit bull ... Bull shit,' the Swede said, and made a gesture, parodying the toreador at the last intrepid moments. Was there a bullfight in the town, he wondered.

'You are not in Pamplona now, Maestro,' D'Arcy said as the Swede repeated bull and shit in a perplexed manner.

'Have you read Groses's *History of Buckish Slang?*' D'Arcy asked and when the Swede shook his head D'Arcy hit him rattily. Objecting to being treated in this lowly manner, the Swede rolled up his sleeves as if to challenge D'Arcy, who parried and said that the cheap drink was rotting their neutrons and why did they not order a decent bottle of good grog, since they were now blessed with female company. From the great array of bottles, a square black bottle was produced. It was wooden, with the wounds of wood painted black and the cork secured by a bright red seal.

'Napoleon's serum,' D'Arcy said as he inhaled it proudly.

Glasses were filled and clinked ceremoniously.

'Cats pyjamas,' the Swede said again, causing D'Arcy to do a study of the man's head, to see if there was a brain in it at all, or if the grey matter had been replaced with goat's pellets. Pummelling and pawing, D'Arcy rejoiced, said the skull bore a strong resemblance to the skull of Robert Burns who as all the world knew had had a pre-neolithic ancestor residing in a cage at Oban.

The madman who had invaded my sleep the first evening sat in a corner, a model of reticence, since it was clear that this night of prodigality belonged to D'Arcy and to D'Arcy alone. Suddenly Iris put her head through the door. She was wearing a black cloak with a russet lace mantilla and her eyes invited adventure. Soon as she saw me she withdrew.

'Who is the veiled sybil?' D'Arcy asked, and ran to call her back. He fell over a table and spilt a bottle of red wine onto a German woman's lap, a faux-pas made worse by the fact that she was wearing shorts and that she did not understand a word of English. The wine ran over her thighs as D'Arcy bent to express his profoundest apologies. Then he ordered her another bottle and decided to regale her with a few lines from Robert Burns –

'ae fond kiss and then we sever . . .
ae farewell, alas! for ever!'

The Swede put down his glass abruptly and went towards the open door.

'Norseman . . . Norseman,' D'Arcy called, terrified that he was going to be landed with an enormous bill. By putting his hand to his flies the Swede indicated that it was the call of nature.

'Paying tribute to Cloacina,' D'Arcy told the German woman and then remarked on the stupidity of the Swede who was wearing a T-shirt that was not only too small for him, but had that most ridiculous of insignias – 'I'm Greta . . . Try me.'

'Greta who . . . Greta fucking Garbo,' D'Arcy said and then pulled me aside, to whisper a word in my ear. I was not to leave, I was not to abandon ship, he had a bit of business up his sleeve, a bit of business that would be better expedited by the ministering and loving presence of a woman. The Swede, he explained, had a wife in Malmo, one Solveig, who was a bit moody, a bit dropsical. He had seen a photograph of her earlier, at lunch-time when they met, and courtesies were exchanged.

'Intelligence has been received that he is loaded,' D'Arcy said and vowed that ere night ended some of that money might end up in our coffers. In due course, we would repair to his studio and I would make finger sandwiches with anchovy paté or strawberry jam or whatever.

Staring across at us was a man with curly brown hair and large grey eyes, like sheep's eyes. It was Scottie, Jnr, the agonized artist.

'That's our Scottie,' D'Arcy said. 'And oh man, he is now awash with freedom after his long night of autocratic sex . . . the truth has suffered to ooze out, wifey followed him hither, so he is enjoying a renaissance of conjugal rites.' Beside him sat a largish woman, busily knitting. D'Arcy commented on her plaits, her flagellating plaits and her hips which he deemed fearsome, and begged me to feel some pity for poor Scottie who had to pretend that he did not know any of those nubile visiting American girls, with the lolly.

The Swede came back, his face splashed with water, tears

flowing from his eyes. Out there, under the moon and the stars he had had a vision; he would sell his sawmill, he would move here and paint orchards.

'Bollocks,' D'Arcy said, and added that there were enough orchards on canvases already, diseased bushes, haemorrhoidal gooseberries and so forth. The Swede envisaged for himself and Solveig a perfect future, they would have picnics on the mountain, fall in love again, live like bohemians. D'Arcy shook his head at such fancifulness and said the Swede was to think one word and that word was timber. The Swede admitted to having troubles, indeed his troubles had sent him hither, it was that or suicide. The factory was losing money, there was labour unrest, his salesmen were drunk by noon, whereupon D'Arcy butted in with a solution – the Japanese technique, the Samurai induction where salesmen learnt the rules. There was a place where salesmen went to learn the Sales Crow Song. He had read about it and now proceeded to indoctrinate the baffled Swede.

'The products you make with the sweat of your brow
You must sell with the sweat of your brow.
The products you make with your tears
You must sell with your tears.'

D'Arcy bellowed it while the Swede tried to repeat it after him.

'Pro . . . duct,' the Swede said heavily.

'Loud . . . louder . . . accurate . . . sincere . . . these are the marks of a true warrior, a true selling Samurai,' D'Arcy said, then stressed the need for inner sincerity. Next he was reciting the businessman's breakfast test.

'A salary man must have breakfast, because without breakfast he will be lacking in health and energy. What happens if a salary man does not have breakfast – he will not be a good salesman. He will get ill and his family will suffer. What is the current condition of the salary man's breakfast – the current condition is that fifty per cent do not have breakfast.'

'Why not?' the Swede asked, at which D'Arcy foamed and

said because they were stupid salary men who would not take the proper instructions from a superior, who would not perform the task as cleverly as a fox, as faithfully as a hunting dog, and as bravely as a lion. For the benefit of the swelling audience D'Arcy enacted the baying sounds of these animals but soon an incensed woman, dressed in an overall, came from the rear of the bar and without having to speak, conveyed to him that he was going too far.

'Descalzas Reales ... my barefoot Princessa,' he said and bowed, assuring her that he would not defile her esteemed posada. There was disdain in her back as she turned away. Japan, D'Arcy then continued, was where the future of mankind lay, the cornerstone of business acumen. He knew it. He had been there once. He had been stupid enough to come home but he would go again, and in a bank in London there was lodged a single ticket to Tokyo which he had purchased some years ago and which, alas, needed refurbishing. He took his hat off and passed it round, and for fun, people put ridiculously small amounts into it, which he tossed onto the terrace. It happened quite suddenly. D'Arcy was dilating on his own plight, his shag-artist plight, on the dreams that scald mankind, when he suddenly happened to say the name Vincent Van Gogh which brought ejaculations from the Swede as he folded his hands and genuflected to Vincent Van Gogh, his brother, his hero, his saint. He believed that he was the reincarnation of Vincent and that one day he would paint like that, the gift would come to him. Moreover, if Vincent were alive now he would be in a five-star hotel, his atelier bursting with tubes of paint, all the canvases he needed, because he, Gunnar Helm, would see to it. His eyes brim with tears as he tells D'Arcy that at moments he is Van Gogh, he has painted those boots, those matted chairs, those wild irises; in his head that is, and now D'Arcy has an arm around him, clutching him, dragging him out of there while at the same time exhorting me to sign the chit, to say we will pay on the morrow.

Down the busy street, careless of motor cars and motor-cyclists, they go, arm in arm, with D'Arcy reciting –

'Caesar and Lepidus take to the fields ... wibbeldy ... wobbeldy ... wu ... Caesar and Lepidus take to the fields ... wibbeldy ... wobbeldy ... wu.' He advises me to wave a kerchief, red or white, as the case may be, to tell all passing cruisers that he and the Norseman have charge of the thoroughfare. Two oncoming cars scream to a halt as D'Arcy puts his head through the open roof of one, asking a disgruntled young man if he has been perusing the cosmos, Venus's pudenda, or the Milky Way's rectum. Taking a short-cut where there is no street lighting, they stagger and fall, regain their faltering balance, all the while D'Arcy assuring the Swede that a meeting such as theirs was made in heaven. We go up some steps, then along a ramp, and he advises me to find the door key by the side of the fonta.

'Enter Holy House of Mecca,' D'Arcy says as he leads us through a room with Turkish cushions and Turkish hangings on the wall. Absurdly, the little round table is laid for breakfast, complete with packages of cereal, marmalade, and a silver and gold coffee pot. He warns us that the good people are in bed. We go down a hall, past some doors, to a room at the end and as he pushes the door open and switches on the light I see a cluttered studio, mostly blue and violet nudes, several musical instruments and a sign in bright red which says, 'Abandon your reason all who enter here.' But the miracle, the *pièce de resistance*, is none of those things, it is a painting on an easel, newly finished, so new that the thick paint is moist. In a light blue jacket and with bristling, upstanding, red-bronze hair is a portrait of Van Gogh, looking like an amalgam of Van Gogh and D'Arcy himself. He is wearing a pair of wide-winged tortoiseshell sunglasses and in the blue lenses are the floating orchards that he painted in the last fevered days of his life. The Swede is speechless. The Swede starts to roar, then he starts to cry. He goes towards it, overawed. He has never seen anything like it. It is a mirage. It is not a mirage. He will pay anything for it. He will pay the ticket to Tokyo and back.

'A weightier sum if you please,' D'Arcy says.

'Excuse me, my English no good,' the Swede says.

'Bollocks,' D'Arcy says, and tells the Swede in King's English, coupled with mime, that the fee is two thousand dollars and that I am at hand to witness it. The Swede grasps the figure, gasps, demurs, halves it, and eventually they agree on fifteen hundred and shake hands.

'It is yours, my warlord, my Samurai, Vincent is now yours...' D'Arcy says; whereupon the Swede proceeds to pick the painting off the easel, but D'Arcy intercepts him.

'Money, my lord ... shekels.'

The Swede explains that due to the perils of travel, highwaymen, brigands and so forth, he never carries such large amounts but that he will go to the bank in the morning and have Solveig wire the money by the afternoon.

'Hath not a Jew eyes ... ears ... heart,' D'Arcy says, putting his hands out in the manner of Shylock. The Swede assures him that he is a man of honour and once again picks up the painting. D'Arcy grabs it, says it is not a matter of commerce, it is simply for art's sake; he wants to add a few finishing touches to it, especially to the revers of Vincent's jacket which is too dun. The Swede insists that he loves the picture as it is, and begs to be let take it.

'It's yours,' D'Arcy says, and to prove it he picks up a brush, dips it in a palette, and writes, 'Sold,' in a vivid blue-green. The Swede erupts, he cannot bear this defilement, this sprawl.

'Vincent wouldn't care,' D'Arcy says, and torn between umbrage and drunkenness the Swede begins to laugh and says, 'Vincent wouldn't care.' Now the two of them are laughing, the bonds of friendship and brotherhood are renewed, as they salute Vincent, the Impoverished One.

Again the Swede tries to grab the painting and grasping it D'Arcy says that he would like to point out, as G. K. Chesterton before him has pointed out, that Irishmen are nifty with the practice of physical assault. They are each holding one end of the painting with D'Arcy shouting, 'Tomorrow and tomorrow and tomorrow.'

'No ... now,' the Swede says.

'No such word Swedenborg ... no now, means never ...

whereas tomorrow ... dawn ... Aurora ... breakfast in your bedroom ... knock-knock ... genii arrive ... I, D'Arcy with painting.'

The Swede wrenches the picture from him and D'Arcy calls on me to bar the door because he intends to beat the bastard to a pulp. He grabs the Swede from the back and pinions him to a wall against the violet nudes. The Swede lets the picture fall as D'Arcy gives him a few preliminary punches. Blood pumps from his nose, and D'Arcy, sobering slightly, and fearing he might have lost the sale, pleads the artist's fifth amendment, which is that he must put the finishing touches to the work before bringing it to the hotel at dawn. Then he dabs the bleeding nose with a rag, says true friendship is always forged through fisticuffs, and tells me with an excess of sentiment – 'Thou knowest that Gunnar, my brother, is an honourable man.'

'Bibulous bastard and onclene beste' is how he describes him after the Swede has gone, and then he orders black coffee, but not the instant puke, because a mammoth task faces him before dawn. A complete new painting has to be done and why, why, because he, D'Arcy, cannot part with said picture, because in that picture lies his soul, his scrotum, the pipe dreams of his life; that picture and he will never be parted. Before morning there will be two Vincents, one bound for Malmo, and the other concealed in his studio, his for life. He pours water from a jug into a metal basin, sinks his face in it, and asks me in God's name to talk to him, to talk to him, to engage him, to keep him from falling asleep.

A clean white canvas is set upon the easel and he starts to smear it lavishly with a yellow undercoat. He paints with a flourish, great bold crazed strokes, as he celebrates in advance, the money in the palm of his hands, the journey to the capital to book a cheap flight to London, collecting his ticket from the vault in Brook Street, returning to Japan and standing beneath the palace where Yukio Mishima disembowelled himself, beneath the foothills of Mount Fuji. It will help exceedingly if I read to him from the Japanese.

It will spur him on. He points to a pile of books between two sedate bookends.

'Anything . . . read anything . . . just don't stop,' he says.

So, it was *White Snowflowers*, *Kanefusi's Hair*, *Brown Mimosa Seed*, *The Cuckoo Bird* and *The Lover-Star's Reprieve*, all night, as D'Arcy envisaged the future with tinctures of sweet rice wine, plum blossom and that wench, herself, one Ming.

'Little voice like a xylophone,' he said as he mimicked her.

'So it's your lady-love,' I said, tentatively. Lady-love! He grunted at the nicety but conceded that all scheming and dreaming on this planet concerned man and woman.

He twirls the brush in the air, he lets lozenges of paint drop on to the canvas, he jokes about the Swede's avoir-dupois, even wonders if in the lenses of the tortoiseshell glasses he should paint different orchards, straggled orchards with blight; wonders if the bibulous bastard would notice.

It was dawn before the second Vincent was completed, clad in his blue jacket, his bristling hair wet as if Vaseline had been smeared over it. D'Arcy put down his brush to rest and suddenly he looked exhausted. He feared for the transaction, what with the daylight and hangover, feared that he had botched it. He saw his windfall disappear, like thistledown. Picking the wet canvas off the easel, he looked at me with a look that was infinitely sad and infinitely resigned, as if admitting that the great windfall had eluded him and that in his perversity he had wanted it to elude him.

'The Tao that can be told is not the eternal Tao,' he said as he went up the hall and hurried outside, presumably to remonstrate with the Swede, to beg.

Eight

The mountains in the early light were soft and misted, pearled orbs, before the day's break. I was setting out to buy lace and wrought-iron candlesticks at the gypsy market in the town, while in another part of my being I was thinking of not going home at all, but drifting, endlessly drifting. I will give the lace and the candlesticks and whatever I buy to my sons, or my friends, or their friends, I thought, as Wanda gabbled away beside me. She was going to collect a friend from the airport and had offered me a lift. Over the weeks I had met her in the shops or in the bar and always she was eager for conversation. I knew by now a little of her past, how she had come there temporarily, only to find that while she was away her husband had gone off with someone else, a dancer from Seville, and the two of them had set up house and a mail-order business in Southern California. Her son kept making tapes which he sent to his father to ask for the money to go to boarding school but as yet there was no answer.

'You'll miss him,' I said.

'I'll miss him,' she said, not really realizing it.

We were the only people out, the lorries full of provisions had not started on their rounds. The air was fresh, iridescent, terraces glowing with light, houses cloaked in their sunny slumbers and churchbells in their niches silent, matt with verdigris. As we drove along the mist lifted from the mountains, like a veil being lifted from a face. Those mountains she was blind to for three years after he left, because of her appalling hangovers. She would stagger out, look at them and, unable to see them, crawl back to bed and bury herself. But that was behind her now. She had had a few romances of course. In this place one met people all the time, people escaping from something or searching for something, people who had dropped out or half dropped out and were as she said smitten by the place, bewitched. There had been several pairs of men's slippers under her bed and endless eyeball-to-eyeball philosophizing, but as she said, before you know where you are, you're cooking for them . . . you're apologizing for your hair being a mess . . . you're begging your kid to call them daddy or at least uncle and just when you think it's all working out, the bastard ups and leaves.

'Is there someone now?' I said, thinking in some other part of my mind that other people's heartbreak does not touch in the same way, simply because we're not prepared to look in at it, at the depths of it. Yes, there was someone but he hardly counted. What am I saying, she exclaimed, there were two or three. More maybe. Somebody else's English boyfriend who rang every day to say he'd like to play tennis or he'd like to pop by to discuss modern art. Modern art! There was of course, *the* guy; he came by bus occasionally, spent the night but as far as she knew lived with a woman on the other side of the island, an older woman, German, hardly ever went out, had phobias.

'So, I play tennis with one and footsie with another . . . but no numero uno or numero dos for that matter,' and she laughed with a twinge of bitterness. When she laughed her gold bridging glinted harshly.

She was recounting a dream she had and was still reeling from. It was of a man who kept all his women, herded, in a dormitory . . . no, not a dormitory . . . more like an institution or a prison. He wore a jock strap and he came over each one but it was ugh . . . it was rusty . . . it was filthy. She, Wanda, was told to go to her cell, at the end of the corridor, and wait there. She would hear the others getting their gout of rust and she was to make herself excited, but not too excited and

wait her turn. Hell, she thought, do I want this, do I want
him ... and turning to me, and in a half-bashful voice, she
admitted that he was someone she knew in everyday life and
hadn't given a thought to.

'What do you make of that?' she said.

'I don't know,' I said.

Something in me recoiled. It was as if she was taking
my own hopes or half-hopes away, hopes that had to feed
themselves on nearly nothing, that clung to spectres. I could
not tell her of the man I loved because to tell her would be
to adulterate my feeling and yet I knew that she ached to
know, the way women do, half in curiosity, half in mischief.
As she dropped me off she wagged a finger and said I was a
secretive one, but that I was not to forget that her apartment
would be vacant in a matter of weeks and that I was top of
the list.

'We'll play gin rummy ... we'll have fun,' she said, giving
me that smile, that coy, girlish smile I knew so well.

The market was not at all as I had envisaged it. It was stall
after stall with a glut of knick-knacks, mostly brass that
smarted in the sun. I had expected something different, the
lace, the wrought-iron candlesticks that Iris had boasted of.
On her last day at the hotel she had got into the pool and
even deigned to talk to another woman. They swam slowly
up and down, in tandem, their heads covered in frilled
bathing caps, their wrists adorned with jewelled watches.
Iris was telling the woman of the bargains she had found at
the gypsy market, the lace, the wrought iron, even a samovar,
an eighteenth-century Russian samovar, can you imagine,
for nothing, for a song. She had even cajoled the little man
into packing it and shipping it to Paris. Marvellous, really,
the things you can do with a bit of coaxing and a bit of
artfulness.

All I could see were varnished wooden caskets and wooden
scuttles of grotesque design, made to look unlike wood, cheap
jewellery and leather bags hanging and swinging from coarse
nails. The gypsy women were laying out their wares and
their flowers. They were strong, well-built, their dark hair

parted severely in the centre and tied back with tortoiseshell slides. The flowers had just been delivered and each one was busy adorning her own stall, and putting flowers into tins and buckets. Here again, lilies, sweetpea, roses, pinks, gladioli, the women seeming not to care whether they had a sale or not, showing an indifference to their customers, almost a disdain. They had an uncanny earthiness as if the high-heeled shoes that they wore were merely plinths which connected them to the earth beneath, not just its surface but to the foundations where the sewer and the sap flowed, way way beneath to the earth's root. Suddenly I saw a figure that gave me a start. It was a young girl, her black hair wet and with a sheen. She was moving quickly, bobbing underneath the awnings of bags and tablecloths made of machine lace. My heart gave a little lurch because I thought she looked like Catalina. I did not want to meet her there, I felt it would spoil things. Each day she left a large fresh bouquet in my room, and often a little one by the bedside table, and when I bumped into her, I thanked her, but that was all. Some reserve had grown between us. Something in her manner had asked me to keep my distance, a fact strengthened by a conversation I had had with the head waiter. I mentioned her name once, said how vivacious she was, how welcome she made people feel. He was behind the bar counter putting bottles on a shelf. I saw him smile behind his glasses, but it was an insinuating smile.

'Yes,' he had conceded. 'She is a very vivacious girl ... also a little tragedienne ... there is one in every village ... our mountain Carmen,' and by his turning to regroup the bottles, I knew that the conversation had come to an end. Yet for me, to know that she was there, to know that she existed was a consolation in itself. In the evenings when I had a drink or two I would allow myself to think of her, as I might a painting or a beautiful garden. I would dwell on her body the way I never allowed myself to dwell on my own, exploring it with invisible hands, invisible eyes, touching her tentatively and without shame. Her skin I would see as the skin of the lilies, fawn, filtered gold, and her breasts like the oranges with perhaps a crescent around them, her arms like little oars from all the work she did, the heaving and the carting, her belly a dome ripe for child and the hair, when it was not wet, like a burning bush. I would see her doing the flowers, or arriving late, or darting through the courtyard with her friends as if they were playing truant. One day I found her ironing her hair in the laundry room and she laughed and said it was the only way to get the crinkles out. Another time she was at the bus stop and I paid her fare but we did not sit together as there was a bit of a squash. The next day, underneath the jug of flowers there was a catalogue from the shop that made beautiful ceramic plates. She had guessed my taste.

I looked again but the girl with the wet hair had vanished and I felt relief. I was in front of a flower-stall where a woman had begun to compile an arc of flowers. First she made the base of green shrub, rather like the base of a wreath and then she began to build bloom after bloom as if she was building in stone or brick, stalk after stalk, each ascension calling for another and still another so that soon it was this pinnacle which would be impossible to sell, since it would not fit inside any house and was too prodigal for any church altar. She talked to herself as she did it. A little man crept by with leaves and branches and without even turning round she shouted at him. He dropped all the branches at her feet and scampered. I ran too. She did not welcome my staring at her.

A bell pealed in the distance and I thought for a moment it was an angelus bell ringing at an awry time. A crowd gathered round the stall in answer to this ringing and I joined them. There she was, in blue jeans and a white blouse looking far more suave than she ever looked at work, in her tracksuit. It was a stall full of junk, bits of iron, bits of lead, stair-rods, bedheads and this one clay-crusted ample bell which must have come from an old monastery and which she was ringing impudently. As she caught my eye I looked away. She was smiling as she amused the assembly by ringing it boldly again and again and to different effect. The stall-owner then snatched it from her and put it down solemnly. She came towards me laughing, her bare arms out in a gesture of supplication. She had been to the fruit market to sell lemons and her hands and arms were full of infinitesimal little cuts, from picking the lemons. She made me look at them, pore over them. To make matters worse her stupid father had climbed up into the trees and had flung the lemons down, damaging many of them, so that instead of earning the esti-mated amount, she had got only half.

'I picked each one of mine, each one, carefully,' she said, 'but he, he just shook the branches and let them fall off.' She rooted in one of the boxes of junk to find casters for her parents' bed. That was why she had come at all, she normally never came to this market, it was for tourists only.

'Like me,' I said.

'You don't sit in the sun ... you hide in your room and write in your journal ... I want to read it,' she said almost contemptuously as she picked up two casters which dripped with machine oil. She haggled about the price, and perhaps dreading that she was going to ring the bell again he wrapped them in newspaper and gave them to her as a present.

We walked on, past stall after stall – chains, leather purses, leather pouches, blouses, tablecloths and still more brass, an affront to the eye in the blazing sun. On one little makeshift table there was an array of nail varnish, each bottle the same colour, a drained unappealing lilac. She stopped and laughed and showed the vendor her overworked nails with not a sight of a cuticle. The woman ignored her. For the most part the vendors took no notice of their customers, they sat with each other, eating and talking, then glancing up slowly if someone asked the price of something. I stopped to buy a picture of a Madonna and Child but when she heard the price she dragged me away. Further along she saw something she liked and winked to show me how one did the transaction. It was a tin plate which had been painted white and had little pink rosebuds on its scalloped rims. Some of the white paint had chipped away and the roses had suffered the onslaughts of rain; these rinsed roses were cheek to cheek, their curves like the round dimpled cheeks of children on Valentine cards.

She wanted it for the little boy.

'What little boy?' I asked.

'My sister's little boy ... Carlos,' she said evasively. Then she picked up the plate, looked at it with utter disdain and began a rapid dialogue with the vendor. I could not exactly follow what she was saying but I knew that she was taunting him. She was asking him, more or less, if he was selling this item or if he had bought it to feed a dog, his own dog or a stray. She put it on her head like a helmet and drew a smile from the more well-to-do owner of the neighbouring stall who was surrounded by grandfather clocks and was busy polishing a brass weight with great vigour. He agreed with her. She said it was useless, belonged on a rubbish heap. She made a gesture to fling it away. She then held the plate forward and in English and Spanish she began to discuss its wretched life, the curs that had eaten off it, the cats that had drunk milk from it, the wind that had made it roll and roll so that its edges were battered, the rain that had washed it again and again and the many other degradations which she would not mention. All this for my benefit, while at the same time herself and the vendor swapped insults and figures. The plate was pitifully cheap but it was clear that the pair of them enjoyed the battle and had even drawn a little audience. Eventually she took some coins from her crinkled white purse and gave them to him and shook his hand and wished him every happiness.

Walking along she carried the plate like a breast shield. Where the stalls ended there were fields full of tall yellow flowers and beyond that a series of high mud-coloured apartment buildings with television aerials, like bird's feet, askew in the air. She knew exactly what we must do. We must go to the centre of the city to a beautiful old-fashioned bar and have coffee and English breakfast. We would have to take a taxi, because wouldn't you know it, her van, which was really her sister's van, had broken down and she had had to take it to the garage. Any profit from the lemons was now destined to cover the repair of the van.

'Bah,' she said, but she was not peeved, just flirtatious,

and full of bravura as she went out on to the main road, whistling for a taxi. As we drove along she pointed out the sights, a school, a hospital, nightclubs, the cathedral, the university where she hoped one day to go.

Walking down the main shopping street, past the boutiques, she showed no interest in the clothes or the furs and only once allowed me to stop to look in a window where there were red, black and amber mantillas spread out like gorgeous webs on which feathered hair slides lay pinioned like butterflies. I wanted to buy some, one for her and one for me, and was about to go in but she would not hear of it. She put her hand on the belt of her jeans and said she had no liking for finery. All that was for other women, different kinds of women, but not her. She would hate herself if she were seduced by such things. I looked at the shop front and thought I would go back alone. There was no number but I hoped that I would recognize it by the cobbled street and the one neon sign for a brand of cigarettes. The restaurant was just open, the waiters unfolding the stiff starched cloths and napkins. We stood at the counter and she ordered espresso and toast. Suddenly a levity overcame her and she suggested that we have cognac with the coffee. The waiter smiled at her indulgently and put the bottle on the counter so that we could lace it ourselves. We sat on high stools drinking this heady stuff while she ordered Croque Monsieurs and said to add some mustard, for the piquancy. There were English papers on the counter and for a moment I thought that I would have to run away. They were a reminder of him. Any heading or any paragraph, though it did not necessarily concern him brought me back to my own surroundings, the thought of him going to work, driving along the Embankment past the houseboats or the bridge with its little girdle of lights, resurrected many moments, sweet or bridling as the case may be, as when he touched my necklace and in doing so touched the very lining of my being, looking at it earnestly, lovingly, his eyes the blue of forget-me-nots; and then another moment, a quite different moment, ugly, knifing, when in the throes of love, he suddenly drew back from me and said, 'You have too much power over me,' and all I could hear was the revving of his car and then the roaring of his engine up the tree-lined street, a fugitive from me.

Catalina was rhapsodizing about their farm, their great estate, how her family did everything themselves, had their own fruit trees, their own olive orchards, their own vegetables, never bought meat, ate only the rabbits and chickens which they reared themselves and which her mother put in the paella. Her pride in it was like the pride of someone who owned dairies, butteries, pantries. She would never leave the land, it was in her blood, it was in her veins. She talked of how she dug the earth in the places where the plough could not reach, on the inclines of the terraces, on the headlands, around the house which they owned on the mountain and where she would one day live. She described the plough that they had bought as if it were a motor car. She is not with me, or rather she is with me and I am the witness to her excitement as she describes putting the seeds in and weeks later the first little leaf, the first little nurseling above the ground. She talks of her father, how he tests her, how he bullies her, how he watches to see her strength ebb, how he cheers when she falters. That very morning when it was still dark and they had hefted the bags of lemons on to the barrow and were bringing them down the path, he let go of his end, hoping the barrow would run away with her, hoping she would stumble and fall, except that she didn't, she clung on.

'Yesterday, when I was ploughing . . . he did the same thing . . . he ran in front of the plough . . . and for what . . . to remove a little white pebble from the ground . . . no bigger than a bead . . . it wouldn't have broken the plough . . . he just wanted to break me . : . he always wants to break me,' she said, and called him monster, actor, emperor, and clown. He was forever challenging her, asking if she could clear a terrace as well as he, if she could grow radishes as well as he, if she could prune orchards as well as he.

'Can I . . . can I . . . can I not,' she said, excited now from the brandy and her surroundings. No sooner had she maligned her father than she felt a need to praise him. Like her, he loved the land, he cherished it, he knew every hectare of it, he knew if a leaf sprouted or if the goats had eaten a bud, it had been in his family for hundreds of years and since he had no son she had to be his son because her sister was ill and moped in bed, crying, sulking.

'So what would I do with nice dresses or mantillas,' she said, but I felt that secretly she had a yen for some of these things. I could picture her, indeed did picture her, in a taffeta dress the colour of fuchsia, tier after tier of it, falling down over her shins, her feet like the gypsies in the strong black court shoes and black stockings, stamping, wherever she trod. On impulse I took off my earrings and laid them on the counter in front of her. She pretended not to see them, chose to ignore what I had done. She was eating toast and the threads of melted cheese laced her lips as she asked the barman, sweetly, to put cognac in our second cup of espresso.

'Have them,' I said.

'I couldn't,' she said. They were long shell earrings mounted on silver and in the sunlight the dark exotic shell took on rivers of colour, as if a rainbow flowed within them.

'Uno,' she said ... 'Uno.'

She took one earring and put it through her pierced ear and I took the other and put it through mine and then she shook her head and her hair as one on the brink of adventure.

'What do you do in the evenings?' I asked.

'In the evenings ...' she said and shrugged, 'in the evenings I milk the goats ... I cook the supper ... I read to my sister's little boy ... I read fairy tales and then he and I fall asleep and we dream of dragons.'

Later I sat in one of the big squares while she went to make a phone call. It buzzed with life. There were men with monkeys on their shoulders, others doing card tricks, and still others stopping people, trying to sell them gold rings or gold watches, ill-gotten goods. Soon as the telephone became free she went into a little booth. Near me, a fat man with a speech impediment sat on a barrel, selling raffle tickets, shouting his wares in a strange, spluttering voice. The sun blazed and emphasized everything, sugar crumbs on a plate which the previous person had left, the white gold of the watch, a parrot on its lead, its greenness seeming to vibrate and emphasize the gravity of the women in black, who like mourners crossed the square in a slow stately way. It was clear by her stance that she was talking to someone whom she enjoyed talking to. She moved about and I could imagine her saying saucy things. When she came back her cheeks were crimson and she bubbled over with excitement. She had borrowed a scooter and would be my chevalier.

'I can take the bus,' I said.

'You don't trust me,' she said in mock indignation.

'I do,' I said, already dreading it because I knew that she would be reckless, that the excitement of a relatively new scooter would be too much for her.

In the garage as she put on the goggles she was already zooming, breasting a Grand Prix. The attendant watched her with fascination. In the tiny room where he sat and made his coffee there were postcards and out-of-date calendars with views of Peru. He had come from there and for thirty years had been resolving to go back, except that he was penniless, and lived as she said in a hen coop in someone's back yard.

'We go together ... Conquistadors,' she told him proudly as they hefted the bike across the garage and out into the sunshine. A certain caution reigned as we manoeuvred our way through the maze of cobbled streets and side streets but once we came up on to the main road she found her momentum. My arms gripped feverishly, holding on to whatever I could, one minute it was the narrow belt of her jeans, the next minute it was her blouse that had ballooned out. I could not decide which was worse, the vertigo, the smell of burning oil or the hot air that rose up from the road. From time to time she shouted words of enthusiasm, asked if I loved the wind or smelt the balsam or whatever. The sea which I saw when she took the corners was an upside-down version of sky, heaving crookedly, like water being sloshed about in a giant beaker. Far out there was a liner, a white liner that seemed to be gliding at a snail's pace. The corners were the worst. Twice she hollered at me as I leant in the wrong direction and caused her to swerve.

'Lean in to the turn ... lean in to the turn,' she shouted, but minutes later she was uttering her satisfaction at everything and said how pleasant it was not to be interned in a car or van, to be one with the wind. I expected us to land into a lorry or a bus and almost wished for it, because at least the ordeal would be over. Farms, gateways, flowers came in mad swoops as if seen from a Ferris wheel at a funfair.

'Smell the pollen, smell the balsam, smell the sea,' she would say, her voice rising above the din of the tappets that were like some out-of-tune, mechanical piano. I saw the high wall on a great swerve of road and thought it was only two more kilometres between life or death, only to be daunted afresh by her suggestion that we speed through the town and spend the day visiting other towns and port towns, enjoying ourselves.

'I can't,' I screamed.

'Why not?'

'I have an appointment,' I said.

She came to an abrupt stop outside the bar, our arrival causing something of a stir. Two girls in shorts sat on the steps and eyed us with a sort of disdain. She looked back at them and suddenly expressed the longing to be in some strange country, alone, free, independent, unfettered.

'Aren't you coming to the hotel?' I asked.

'It's Saturday ... I don't work Saturday or Sunday,' she said.

'Maybe you would like to have dinner,' I said on the spur of the moment.

'You'd be bored,' she said. 'I'm a peasant ... I'm an ignoramus,' and a line came to me out of the blue – 'Her heart amber and plump' – but she was already gone, leaving me with the anxiety that I was unsporting, and that I lacked daring.

Nine

The driveway was long and winding. At times, it seemed like a well-kept private road, then deteriorated into a track, with old trees and old tree stumps out of which briars sprung. The taxi driver kept turning round to voice his displeasure. I had been summoned by Iris and since it was a doleful Sunday, I agreed to go. Soon as I heard the dogs barking and as the car swerved in front of a large house, I guessed it was the right place. The dogs were behind gates, but on the lawn itself a flock of peacocks, strutting, their ghostly cries in contrast with their blue-green plumage, which at that moment splayed expansively.

An upstairs window was opened, and Iris called out in a summary fashion that I was to keep the taxi. I walked about, wondering whether or not a maid would admit me. At either side of the big bevelled door were two huge pieces of olive wood, like replicas of a neolithic man and woman, guarding the entrance. The taxi driver made no secret of his impatience, and I stood, of two minds, wondering whether to touch the brazen knocker or to wait.

Eventually she appeared. She was not wearing a coat, not even a dress, and to my surprise she looked dishevelled. She was wearing a long purple slip and her feet were bare. She gave me a little peck on the cheek and said that she would like to show me the house, or at least the courtyard, that I must see the roses, the roses were the only reason she had rented the place.

'He's in a bad mood,' I said, pointing to the taxi. She ignored that, and I followed her through a dark shuttered hallway and then through vestibules also dark, into a huge courtyard where there were indeed masses of roses. They hung in bunches, in clusters, great traunches of them trailing over low-tiled roofs, covering window casements and in one place blotting out a window completely. The place had a sad, neglected quality.

Soon we went inside and up a stairs to the first floor, because she said that the gallery was one of the features of the house and several centuries old. It was a long narrow gallery that looked out on to the courtyard and it was filled with chairs, many of them brown rocking chairs. For some reason, I imagined invalids sitting there looking out at the beautiful roses, plaintively. I did not want to be there, I wanted to be with Catalina, I yearned to be with her, on the scooter, on her farm, milking the goats with her, anything because here in this deserted and luxurious place there were whiffs of despair, reminding me too pointedly of my own life.

By the way she staggered I saw that Iris was not well and that possibly she had been drinking. There was no music playing, no other voices, no sign of her South American house-guest and no murmur of servants. We went through salon after salon, in which there were huge paintings either of animals or gouty ancestors; then long bog-oak sideboards on which there were laid single things such as a chafing dish or a ladle or a set of teaspoons. I kept admiring it, even though I found it dismal. We arrived at the end room which was a little library where a wood fire had been laid. She went towards the telephone and spoke a message into the answering machine which was next to it. She said that she was out, said it twice in a muffled voice and then rooted for the little pad to find the number of the restaurant to which we were going. Unable to find the pad she quashed the message, lost her temper, opened several drawers of the desk, found some book matches with the name of the restaurant and then proceeded to use the machine again. But first she said she needed a drink.

'Get me a vodka ... on the rocks,' she said and pointed to a bar, or at least a tray of drinks in the adjoining room. The dulcet voice had gone and there was, instead, this abrasiveness. Yet as she taped her message she resummoned her seductive tones and said in the nicest voice that she was out, then gave the exact time while she would be in the restaurant and the approximate time when she would be home, begging the caller to allow fifteen minutes in each instance for her to get to and fro. She blew a little kiss. I thought I heard the car drive away but then decided that he was merely turning round and anyhow I felt too nervous to worry her. She donned a long satin dress, which buttoned all the way down, and seemed excessively chaste. From her handbag she took her make-up pouch and painted her lips hurriedly. Her shoes she hauled from under a chair. They were very high-heeled, suede, mauve shoes, with an ankle strap and I could not see how she was going to navigate in them. I was not certain what she was saying as she bent to put the strap through the diamanté buckle, but it was clear she was repeating something that enraged her, something the paramour had said – just give me time, give me time to think, all I need is time to sort myself out, you know I love you, I hate to do this to you, I hate myself for doing this to you, Iris, baby, you don't deserve this ...

She raised her head and looked at me bitterly as if I were the cause of it or in some way a reminder of it. Her South American friend had gone, and where had he gone, to Cannes, and why had he gone, because there was a film festival there, and whom did he hope to meet, cheap little bitches, starlets, pseudo-starlets, models, tarts, the lot. The memory of it, and the knowledge that he was there at that very moment, flattering God knows who, made her demand another drink and this she did by picking her glass up and shaking the ice on to her lap, on to the dress which was only half-buttoned. She pouted like a child.

By the time we came out it was dusk and there was no car. He had indeed gone, my hearing had not deceived me. She fumed. She said how had he gone without being paid. I

88

explained that I had paid him as we came up the drive, as I was under the impression that I was having supper in her house. She almost struck me. Does one have a cook on Sunday evening when one is renting a villa. Where did I get such Pollyanna ideas. One was lucky if one got breakfast. In her high heels she flounced back in and picked up the phone in the hall. She couldn't remember the numbers of any of the taxis so she sent me upstairs to find them. I met her as I was coming down with two printed cards, a fresh glass, a wine glass in her hand, curses issuing out of her, at me, at taxi drivers, at the country she happened to find herself in, at the whole costly mess of it. She was paying a fortune for this place, a fortune for those imbecilic servants, and what was it, a morgue, a morgue, with syphilitic ancestors on the walls and a phone that went out of order every time you blinked. No wonder he'd left. It wasn't her he'd left, it was this cursed house, and she slammed the phone back and said there was nothing for it but to rustle up something and so we went together to the kitchen which was down the main stairs and then another series of narrower stairs. It was a big white kitchen fitted with every kind of equipment and my first thought as I heard all the machines hum, was that I was in a kind of hospital. She opened the refrigerator and took out two pitiful strips of parched veal which looked to have been there for days.

'Vienna schnitzel,' she said, laughing, and then as she went across to the very modern stove she hit her head on the several baskets and copper pans that hung from the low ceiling.

'I give up . . . I simply give up,' she said, almost admitting to tears. It was up to me. I had let the idiot taxi driver go. I hadn't told her he had been paid and was therefore itching to escape, so I had better take my nice tailored jacket off and get down to business. She said she had better explain that none of the pepper mills worked and that if I thought of making a wonderful salad *chaud* to think again because there wasn't any endive in the house, or goat's cheese and possibly only some wilting lettuce.

'There's these,' she said, as from a cupboard she took a stack of tins and plunked them on the white table. She would of course help me but first she must go and erase her message and turn the machine off because she was expecting not one call, but several. She had rung everyone, literally everyone, even her masseuse in Aspen, Colorado, to come and bail her out.

'I'll be back,' she said, very sweetly now, fearing perhaps that I might desert her, that once her back was turned I might creep up the stairs out the door.

I searched in the pantry and found a few things, onions, olive oil, herbs, and then took a long time in choosing one of the many pristine copper pans. I felt quite pleased to be cooking again and thought with a little rush of irrational pleasure what it would be like when I got home. I heard her once or twice but it must have been as she tripped over something or spoke to herself because the phone had not rung and neither had a light flickered, as it would if she had been ringing someone.

It took her so long to appear that I thought perhaps she had gone to bed. I would look at the kitchen clock which was a drained white like separated milk and I would think, 'In another five minutes she will appear,' and then I would squeeze a little more lemon on the cooked veal, which was already shrivelled. When she did come she was beautifully dressed and beautifully made up and there was a freshness to her as if she had just wakened, as if all her annoyance and disappointment had been whisked away. She wore a different dress, it was velvet, burgundy coloured, and she had long earrings to match, which when she moved actually bobbed against her shoulders. In the most girlish voice she asked me to please forgive her, to please please excuse such awful tantrums, such awful breeding, such unforgivable behaviour and to put it down to a woman, who when she had her migraines lost her marbles. She praised the dinner, said it was delicious, ate masses of the toast and said that we could patent the recipe for the tinned beans, because whatever I had done, they were *très bon*. Then she confided that she also

was a good cook, something of an adventuress with the sauces
and that when she lived in New York she insisted sometimes
on doing her own cooking and made all those hatchet host-
esses green with envy. She asked if I had been enjoying
myself in the hotel, if I had made friends, found lovers, or
at least somebody very *simpatico* and before I could reply
she was shaking her head at her own luck, almost too good
to be true. She was staring into space with that fixed and
pensive gaze of hers, which had become second nature and
which she knew flattered her immensely, gave her the look
of a graven mystic. Her eyes were narrow and she blinked
feverishly as she recalled the wonderful weeks she had had
since she last saw me, so much fun, so much pleasure.
Sorrow, rejection, loneliness, these were things she knew
nothing about. She had of course quarrelled with lovers
from time to time, especially Renaldo, her South American,
because he was so fiery, so tempestuous, naughty boy, but
then ten minutes later he was in her arms and they were
doing a tango, all over the house, upstairs through the salons,
into the garden, like midsummer's night dreamers. He was
the most thoughtful of men, he always made up first, he was
the one to ring straight away, to ring from downstairs if she
had gone to her bedroom in a flounce, to beg, to plead, and
as for flowers he sent them every day, did I not see, did I not
notice those great arrays of flowers. She had had roses, actual
roses, not the Interflora muck, roses from South America,
and no bouquet had ever looked so ravishing. They had
lasted weeks, weeks, they just would not die. In fact, come
to think of it, she should order her flowers from South
America in future and save herself a packet of money.

'I'm so lucky,' she said and gazed ahead at some point in
the reaches of the long dining room, as if the gilded mirror
could absorb an image of her pensive, but exquisite self. Yes,
she was spoiled, she had to admit it, spoiled by men, spoiled
by everyone and moreover she could eat anything, she could
stuff herself and not put weight on. To prove this she took
a piece of toast in either hand and ate each piece alternately,
gobbling as a child would. We drank and talked but all the

while she kept fidgeting and when it struck eleven from the very white clock on the wall she jumped up and asked to be excused. This was when he rang, and they had their cuddles, so wonderful, so exciting, so naughty, almost as if he was in the room, undoing his robe, and they were about to do the Cuadro Flamenco.

'Oh I feel quite randy,' she said, and put her hands to her lips, shocked at her own indiscretion.

'You will let yourself out,' she added, sweetly, non-chalantly as if we were in the middle of a metropolis. Then she told me to be sure to leave my London address because she wanted to dine with me and take me to the opera.

Each time that she was not using the phone I took the opportunity to ring a taxi rank, and each time I got a ringing tone. Then, soon as I replaced the receiver, the red light appeared again and I knew that she was trying to reach him. By midnight I had reconciled myself to spending the night there. I thought I would go upstairs and knock on her door and ask which room it might be suitable to lie down in. But when I went upstairs I hesitated, because I could hear her talking to someone, spelling his name very slowly and clearly, asking the operator to please try his room again, because she knew he was there, he must be.

There was a screen around her bed, a lacquered screen with pictures of birds and simpering ladies. I drew back, and repaired to the study where I had seen a sofa and some plaid rugs.

Sleep would not come, because I yearned to be in my own room in the hotel and because I was cross with myself for having been enticed. I had met women like her before, and they had frightened me, their brittleness, their heartlessness had made me cower. On the tape machine I listened to the voice of Maria Callas, the haunted, liquid voice that I loved, and worried that it might be too loud, I pressed some button, and then suddenly there was another voice altogether in the room, a young man, speaking desperately, calling, 'Mother, Mother.' I started, thinking someone had come in, but the voice was indeed from the machine.

'Mother,' it began ... 'Are you listening ... I hope so, because I want to get it all out. I have followed you around the world to say this, but what did you always do, you fled, you hid, you ran. You were so busy, mother, with your lovers, your secretaries, your dressmakers, your charities, your friends, and your art collection, so busy that when I came home from school at Christmas, I would find my presents on my bed, when each time I hoped, I prayed, that you would hand them to me, but no, there they were, the camera, the watch, the bottle of shampoo with my very own name on the label. But where were you, where in fuck's name were you. The housekeeper, the French one, or the Italian one, or the Colombian one, would always say that you were due back, you had been to lunch, but then after lunch you were tired and in need of your siesta, and then it was tea-time and whats-their-names were coming, people you didn't really know but who might be useful, some dope that owned a museum in San Miguel or Lucca and then some earl was taking you to drinks at six and you would have to get into one of your creations. You had so many creations they would fill the Titanic. I can see them, smell them, those sweeping gowns of yours. I gave a scarf once to a girlfriend and you saw red ... I had to go and humble myself and ask for it back, I had to lie and say it was not yours, it belonged to the Colombian. You bitch. Of course you would phone me in the early morning and ask how I had slept ... Coo-Coo-Coo-Coo. Ask what I would like for breakfast ... ask me in a smattering of French and English ... reminding me that I could have anything so long as it did not have to be cooked ... I could have toast or bran muffins ... fuck your muffins mother ... hey ... listen why don't *you* do it ... go on, have the courage. It's simple. I got the booklet. I swotted up on it and this is what you do ... you down the bottles of vino ... get the good stuff and then your bottle of nembutals ... you have them ... I know ... you send for them specially to that chemist in Horsham, he gives you one hundred at a time and you hoard them like you hoard jewels. Splash out, mother dear, splash out ...'

Here the tape slid and there were only slurps, as presumably he drank. Then the voice resumed except that it was softer, contrite – 'Oh Mother I am sorry to leave you but I hate life . . . what have I ever done . . . nothing. Whatever I did you sneered at it. Do you know *The Seagull* by Chekhov? You must know it. You must have seen it often, there is a mother like you and a son like me. He goes down on his knees to her, he begs. All I ever wanted was to do something to make you proud of me . . .'

When the voice took up again, it was hazed, lost, already half dead: 'Too late, Mother . . . it's working, eight cans of Special Brew and now the last fistful of pills . . . if only I knew where you were . . . are you out at some party . . . or are you having an evening in . . . your TV supper on a tray . . . I saw you this morning in the patisserie . . . I wanted to run to you . . . Too late . . . It's working. Maybe you will come through the door . . . maybe you will and I'll be pumped . . . all I wanted was time . . . Ti . . . me . . . Dar . . . ling . . . Daaarrr . . . ling . . . Mothhhhhh . . . er.'

The cassette had Iris's name written in capitals, was dated the previous June and was signed

'YOUR EX-SON ANDY'

– as if he had just stepped into the room, I felt a shiver. I imagined him pale, thin, I even imagined he had blond hair and blond eyelashes.

The moment it was light, I stood in the landing, outside her room, waiting, for her. She came out, calling the servants.

'Conchita . . . Conchita . . . Pepe . . . Pepe.'

When she saw me she realized that something was amiss and asked if I had seen a ghost, adding that the house was supposed to have the statutory ghost, a woman no less who had drowned herself in the artificial lake. I wanted to embrace her but somehow her coldness and her cleverness were deterring me. Half of me was saying, 'Go ahead and tell her,' while the other half was apologizing for having spent the night. I kept rehearsing it, I even saw her drop her defences and weep, telling me some key moment as where she was when she heard it, when the news was broken to her and who she turned to.

'I played some tapes,' I began to say.

'Don't you love Callas . . . don't you love that sleepwalking aria . . . her trance,' she said.

'Another tape came on . . . a young man's,' I said. She stiffened. All seemed havoc for a moment, the very centre of her being smashed, and rage issued from her like the vapour from erupting lava. She knew.

'Pepe will take you home,' she said and she called loudly, harshly, like a street vendor. I could see clearly her terror, her blue vitreous eyes, the bone of her nose aquiver, her morning gown of voile, and I thought that if I could say it, something tender would occur between us and the stone inside her would dissolve. I thought of those bloods of martyrs in churches in Italy which though solidified do turn to liquid one day a year. The prayers of the faithful cause them to melt. All that was needed was faith. Even as I tried I knew that I could not take those few but immeasurable steps between me and her, between me and life, and that in two or three minutes I would be gone, dispatched, and rubbing her hands she would order breakfast and shout out to herself – 'Imbeciles . . . that's what people are . . . liars . . . imbeciles . . . ogres' – and walking to the breakfast room she would snap off the dead heads of the roses and think that in the future she must be more careful, she must take precautions, because one must, one simply must protect oneself from people, horrid, prying, inquisitive, thieving, stupid, callous people.

Ten

A wind was rising and along the road various boughs and branches had fallen. The driver did not speak, just exclaimed from time to time, said, 'Sirocco ... Sirocco,' and chain-smoked. As I got out of the car the wind whipped about my feet, its howl like the combined and furious seas of the world, while within it there was another sound, a shriek, as of doomed newborn infants.

In the hotel lobby, various telephones were ringing but no one answered them as both the desk and the switchboard were unattended. It was still quite early. The very young sleepy waiter rushed in, jumped over the bar counter, grabbed a bottle of brandy and ran out again. I followed him as he hurried up the steps towards the pool. The wind had ripped the plants out of the terracotta pots so that they lay with clods of clay littered over the steps, along with shards and splinters; the fallen pots on the ground like great neolithic carcasses. I could hear voices and commotion.

A small crowd including some guests and some staff were huddled around a woman who was holding a little boy in her arms, talking to it, talking in a strange voice, as if hypnotizing it. It was the German woman whom I knew slightly, who wore a different bikini day after day, had a blue celluloid sunshade over her eyes and frequently asked her husband to oil her back. She was holding the little boy, Otto, in her arms, talking to him. He looked safe, like a sheaf inside the big towel but by her talking I knew that he was not safe.

Around them were several people, including her husband, who fingered his wide bronze moustache as he kept saying, 'We try to watch him, we try,' hideously mixing past and present because it was clear from all the faces that the little boy was lifeless. The mother was speaking to her child, praying, waiting for his eyes to open, his pulse to beat again, his heart to start thumpety-thump. But the men knew it was all over, the waiters knew, and the father knew, because they had given him the kiss of life, they had done everything they could after the mother dragged Otto from the deep end and brought him to the metal ladder, screaming help in three languages.

'He try to do what his sister do,' the father said to the waiters, to the bystanders and now to me. The storm had wakened the little boy, the clatter of things breaking and rattling had wakened him, unduly early. He had crept out of his cot while they were still asleep and had gone down with his water-wings to the pool, had got in, believing somehow, in his dazed state, that his sister or his father or someone would follow. His sister stood looking up at her mother, expecting a miracle. She was holding a box of crayons which someone must have given her along with a jotter. Most of the people were in their nightdresses with coats over them, which they clutched in the wind, but the mother was naked as the towels slipped, though the head waiter again and again tried to put them back in place. She threw them off, not knowing what she was doing, begging her husband to give Otto life, to bring it back while all the while her husband pleaded with her to take brandy from a spoon. On the ground were the blue and red water-wings, one squelched and the other flat. So this was the little boy that I saw day after day, witnessed his pranks: he would stand on the first step of the ladder with his blue and red water-wings already donned, simulating fear, doing oohs and aahs until his sister, Greta, lifted him in. He would call in his high childish voice ... Greta Greta, and soon as he was in, he wanted to get out again, then ran to his mother or father to dry him and then back to the ladder to simulate the fear and do oohs and aahs until his sister lifted him in. The mother is speaking to Otto, half speaking, half singing, in a coaxing voice. When the coroner comes she breaks down completely, describing it in broken English, searching for the words and somehow finding them, the words that tell that she cannot face it, that she does not believe it and that something must be done. She tells how in her sleep she heard the wind, she heard the voice of her little boy, the soul of her little boy crying, 'Mama, mama,' and she wakened, looked, saw the empty cot, the covers thrown off, ran, and as she says all this, she is clutching the shirt front of the coroner who is a solemn man and sad-looking, sad no doubt from what he's called to do day after day, dawn after dawn. As she is talking, he is trying to write things down but impeded by her assaults. He alternates in her mind between friend and enemy, because at some moments she is talking calmly to him, reasonably and at others she is shouting as if it is his fault, as if he has come to accuse them of being negligent, of not loving their little boy; then she screams as she relives the run she made, down the stairs, down another stairs, across a courtyard and a shrub garden and to the pool where she does not need to look; she jumps in and finds her little boy and it is as if he is not dead, he is sleeping, he is trailing . . . 'He is not dead, he is sleeping,' she roars it, for all to hear, and her husband puts his hand gently across her mouth, his ringed marriage finger looking absurd in this light, in this crisis. Her husband takes up the evidence for the coroner. There is something barbarous about the fact that it is all being written down, her waking, her running, her jumping in, her swimming back up, her relief that her little treasure is not dead, even though he is dead. He describes his own running to the scene, meeting a waiter on the way, the two of them assisting his wife, laying Otto out – he can hardly say the name – on the grass, trying to revive him with the kiss of life. He looks at the waiter with immense and useless gratitude as he says these things, then he too breaks down but he checks himself and puts an arm, a needful, comforting arm around his little daughter and says wretchedly, 'Otto try to do what his sister do.'

A young policeman arrives, shy and unshaven; he stands next to the coroner as if that is the proper thing to do. They are trying to take the sheaf from its mother, begging her to move from the spot, as if by moving she will feel less demented, she will admit the fact that it has happened and that it cannot be made to unhappen. I think of Iris with a mixture of rage and pity. What would she do if she were here; would she break down? Suddenly and to everyone's surprise the mother hands Otto over, like a little parcel and then possessed of a whim of modesty she draws the towels around her and looks at me and shakes her head. I shake my head in return. We used to have conversations about the room we went to each week, to have our hair done, a make-shift place, the owner's sitting room, where she used to have to carry the bowls of hot water in from the kitchen. We joked about it once, how primitive it was. The father carries the little boy and walks off up the steps not knowing quite where he is going. The head waiter tries to disperse the added crowd, some to weep, some to watch, some to mutter about how careless the parents had been. Most of all they watch the mother, the gnashing mother who cannot believe that it has happened because it is a ghost happening, a ghost death, there is no grave to mark the actual spot where her little boy went down, down into that pocket of water that is no longer there, dispersed as it is by other pockets of water and even as we look we hear cruelly the plop-plop as through the vents fresh water issues, bubbling, gurgling, indifferent; as is the cold windy surface with its impersonal little pleats.

Suddenly she is berserk again. She refuses to follow the cortege. By following she will have to admit that she is being parted from her little boy, whom in life, day after day, second after second, she took for granted.

'I can have no more child,' she says, grasping the coroner's arm.

'You can,' a woman says.

'I can have no more child,' she says and the woman tries to comfort her by saying that God wanted him, that God

wanted her little boy very much. She reacts to this with such
rage, such frenzy it seems for a moment that she is going to
claw the woman's eyes out. She lifts her hands, draws them
down over the woman's face as if putting a curse on her or
else transferring the curse that she feels has been put on
herself. She runs after them, snatches the infant back, shouting and keening over it, bringing her face to it, breathing,
whispering, even putting it again at her cold breast to suckle.
Her husband pulls her away, not quite so gently now, as the
head waiter tells the crowd that it is best to leave them, it is
best to leave them alone to grieve.

We watch them walk away, a tableau of mourners and
officials. Up to then, they were a German family who had
brought their breakfast charcuterie down to the pool and
picnicked, now suddenly they are the pitiable ones who have
lost their little boy. The storm makes it worse, adds to the
calamity, a hectic wind blowing things about, oranges fall
through the air in a mad flourish and the stalks of flowers on
the ground are oozing a white stuff. Someone says that the
family are going back to Germany to bury Otto, are driving
straight away to catch the ferry. There is no way that one
can imagine that drive, past ravaged fields, roads strewn with
boughs, past strange towns, through a land where they must
feel that fate had crushed them.

Later the head waiter came among us and asked us if we
would be so kind as not to tell newcomers since it might put
a damper on their holidays. Without his glasses, his eyes look
hurt, not the hurt of the moment, but a bigger hurt. Then
he rallied, looked at his big pocketwatch made of silver, and
ordered the waiters about and soon they carried baskets of
breakfast to the various rooms, to the people who had slept
through the tragedy and the others who had gone back to
bed.

'How long will the sirocco last?' I asked the head
waiter.

'One day, two days, three . . . who knows . . . maybe you
never go home . . . maybe you are marooned here,' he said
without laughing.

The poplars swayed like drunken reeds, poplars that would serve as wands to the unknown spot within the depths of the pool where little Otto had gone down.

Eleven

Catalina had not come nor was there the usual heap of flowers on the table for her to arrange. The table itself had turned over. I stood in the courtyard looking at things, broken pots, ripped off petals and severed cacti that looked like disembodied crocodiles, waiting for her, eager for her as if her appearance alone would dispel the morbid gloom. Even the hotel had lost some of its harmony, some of its allure, people skulking about half fearing a fresh catastrophe. Eventually, when she did not arrive I decided to go to her house, even while realizing that such a thing was precipitate. One of the other maids gave me instructions on how to get there, reminding me that there was her house and her grandmother's house, both bearing the same family name, but that her grandmother was very odd, shied away from people and was thought by some to be a witch.

Along the street people saluted or attempted to salute as they soldiered along or ducked to avoid a falling clatter of roof tile or gutter. Children ran about in outlandish clothes – curtains and tablecloths which they wore as togas. They were uttering some wild chant. It was an Arab chant in keeping with the sirocco.

'Shish-Kal-Abaam, Shish-Kal-Abaam, Shish-Kal-Abaam,' they said in a shrill chorus.

A little group had gathered around one of the big houses and in the courtyard two huge white Alsatians were pacing and moaning. Here too, tragedy had struck.

'Poor Walter ... poor dear,' Wanda said, pointing to the open door, through which I could see heavy brown furniture and vases of madonna lilies, which, having fallen down, looked weirdly libertine. Walter, one of the visiting Americans, he who days before, in the crowded bar, had boasted that the only thing that mattered to him was partying and that he would party with anyone, had had a heart attack. He had come down on to his terrace, like many another, to carry his plants in, when suddenly he keeled over and might have lain there to die but that his dogs raised the alarm by the ominousness of their howls. An ambulance had been called and he was being carried away on a stretcher, his dogs fretting; his boyfriend bulky, sullen, impassive. His boyfriend had not come home the previous night, had been playing cards in the next town.

'Poor Walter,' Wanda said again and raised her eyes, implying that the heart attack was the result of unrequited love and not partying.

A woman, whom I had never met before, invited me to have coffee and as I went through the door I recognized the Turkish hangings and the coffee pot.

'Doesn't D'Arcy work here?' I said.

'Work!' she said, admitting an impatience that was masked by infinite restraint and forbearance. D'Arcy had helped her husband to cast some sculptures, then had forgotten to leave, but he had promised to move out soon. As we sat there, eating currant biscuits and drinking very strong coffee, she talked about the winters, the damp, how she would like to go away in the winter, live in a big city and frequent the cinemas in the afternoon. The place was a paradise, true, but the winters wet and long and lonely.

'Maybe paradise is lonely,' I said to cheer her. She had this wounded quality as if at birth she had heard only one command – 'Thou shalt go forth into the world and be a slave.'

The front door burst open as the group of crazed children came in and circled round us, shouting – 'Shish-Kal-Abaam, Shish-Kal-Abaam.' Two of them were her children, changelings out of place in the neat sad room. I excused myself on the grounds that I had to make an urgent telephone call and she stood in the doorway to try and detain me by reminding me that due to the storm, the wires were down.

It was like walking through a heated void. The wind still thrashed and keened and in the distance I could hear the cocks crowing deliriously which added to the displacement of things. The street was deserted and the road looked violated – carob pods strewn about like green bandaging, overturned dustbins and new tar in little heaps like oily turds. They had tarred a patch the day before. I went down the donkey path, and along the road, past the dried torrent and over the bridge towards her house. Two acacia trees, like bridal trees were in full flower, except that much of the blossom had fallen off and lay like limp garlands on the ground.

I could hear shouting as I approached her gateway and I was about to turn back but I met a young girl who introduced herself as Catalina's sister, Rosario, and she told me to go on down, thinking perhaps that I had brought some message, some reprieve from the hotel. She was thin and shrewish, had none of Catalina's sheen or verve.

Through the open door I saw Catalina wielding a knife, then cutting bread in a businesslike fashion. A man, presumably her father, sat at the table, hunched but combative. He was waving a letter in his hand, a letter typed on official paper. She was different here, unwashed, unkempt, scruffy, bawling like a hyena. The kitchen itself was quite dark and full of clutter. Her father was the first to see me and as soon as he did he composed himself, raised an eyebrow without raising the lid and made a finicky movement with his little finger, as if to say, what a tawdry place I had chanced on, what a hovel. She turned, surprised to see me. She had put gel in her thick black hair so that it stood up in great swathes and I could see that she was incensed. I heard myself mutter that I had been passing by, knowing that it was an idiotic thing to say. She rallied and in a sudden gesture of hospitality lifted a dishcloth and from underneath took a little tin cup

that was filled with warm custard. She handed it to me, along
with a buckled metal spoon.

'Eat . . . eat,' she said, as if that was why I had come, as if
starvation had driven me in. Its over-sweet yet bland taste,
its little curdles, its golden sugared crust brought to my mind
the custards of long ago, when one was ill with measles or
fever. A little boy stood near her, protecting her, stroking
one spot on the calf of her leg, stroking it endlessly, round
and round.

Knowing how I liked tea she put the kettle on, still sparring
with him, matching every outburst and every fist of his with
her own, emphasizing her fearlessness by standing near him,
or prodding him with the end of a toasting fork, then returning to the stove and refusing to accept whatever barb he had
just issued. At one point she ran and poured hot water on to
the crown of his balding head and I thought then he would
strike her. A woman, obviously her mother, came in carrying
three eggs in her hand and by her expression seemed to say
she was surprised that hens could lay eggs in a storm such
as this. She held them out to Catalina as if to proclaim a
miracle, as if they had been propelled from the hens' back-
sides by the havoc of nature. They were very white eggs.
Because of where I was standing, she had not seen me, but
the moment she did she gave me a suspicious look that said
I had no business being there. She looked alarmed. I thought
maybe she believed I had some connection with the hotel
and had come to bring Catalina to work. Catalina spoke to
her rapidly and in a low voice and I knew she was explaining
who I was and how she knew me. The mother looked at
me again with a greater scrutiny, thinking probably of the
privileged life I had, being able to travel, being able to stay
in a hotel, my hands smooth, not like hers which were worn
and gnarled. Then she picked up two buckets and hurried
out, presumably to fill them with water. A cat ran about
the kitchen, rasping, looking under chairs, so much so that
Catalina broke off from her duel, to explain that the kittens
had been drowned that morning. They sparred and sparred,
and either out of nervousness or to draw attention to himself,

the little boy pulled his pants down and a great soft explosion of shit gushed from him.

'Diarrhoea ... diarrhoea ... my god,' Catalina screamed, while in a gesture of disdain the father held his nostrils together and gave me a curious flirtatious smile. Catalina ran, returned with a bucket of water which she sloshed on the floor and then began to sweep vigorously.

'It's all crazy ... crazy,' she said, her way of both apologizing and appealing to me. I stepped outside to avoid the splashes and waited, half wondering if I should go. The storm was abating and the sound of the wind now a heave, like the heave of a sated monster. The yard looked ravaged, fallen branches, fallen fruits, and the hens and ducks huddled together in earth baths, too frightened to move. Some toy trucks stuck up out of a bed of sand and I thought how she must have gone down to the sea and fetched it up. Hearing the row regain momentum, with now the mother's voice as well, I decided to leave. She caught up with me at the gate and thrust something in my hand.

'I've had it for years,' she said.

I looked down and saw a painted wooden blue eye, a protection against evil. The blue had been bleached by time or else she had worn it when she swam.

'But it's your lucky eye,' I said.

'Don't lose it,' she said anxiously.

I loved her then, regardless of her unwashed body, her hair smeared with gel, loved the impulse that wanted to give me something, to make up for the absence of hospitality in the house.

'I had to come,' I said and she touched my shoulder, in a gesture of affection and forgiveness.

'I'm glad,' she said but presently she was running back towards the house, in answer to a fresh challenge. This time it was her mother, calling, and walking towards her with the incriminating letter. For some reason I imagined it was about money.

Twelve

I got there early in case she decided to cancel. I dreaded the first moments when she would arrive, the clumsiness, not knowing what to say. It was Sunday, her day off and I had reserved for lunch in another restaurant, under the mountain and overlooking the sea. Although it was daylight the moon still lingered in the heavens, it was not amethyst as D'Arcy had once predicted but a grey pock-marked embryo that shamed itself by being there. The light was shockingly, searingly bright, so bright that the cones in the undersides of the cypress trees stood out like very white knuckles, clear enough to be counted or to be smacked, one by one.

Geraniums festooned the surrounds, coral coloured, flagrant like cockscombs, tumbling out of terracotta pots, the incarnation and the emanation of a redness that was not fire or flame but rather like a powder, a primordial rouge altering whatever it touched. Likewise the roses, thrilled and thrilling, the whole garden agog, the laid tables like altars waiting for their rite.

The water down below was a bright fidgety blue, but in two places it was green where the roots of the two huge guardian rocks cast a shadow that had the amorphousness of cloud. Although I was expecting to see her come up a tall flight of steps, she came from the back through the garden, an apparition, a picture of radiance, herself a flower, a lotus, unfolding. It was as if the verve and prodigality of the geraniums had infected her. She wore a tapered, feathered earring, a white openwork blouse, and her pink muslin skirt had so many linings, it looked like foam.

'I'm five minutes late,' she said, shyly.

The various waiters knew her and complimented her; and the head waiter drew a vessel with his hands to show the outlines of a shapely woman. His wife, she whispered, was the local dressmaker, very fat, always complaining that her stomach was not like her clients' stomachs and wondering why this was so. She said that we would swim first, in order to get a big appetite.

'I won't,' I said, too embarrassed to tell her that I couldn't swim.

'You must,' she said, doing a little pout.

'Tomorrow,' I said.

'Tomorrow,' she said, and she was already removing her lace blouse, to show a knitted pink swimsuit underneath.

She ran down the steps and along the overgrown path calling to one of the dogs to come with her. I saw her, then lost her, then saw her again as she got into the sea, a mermaid being carried away towards the patches of blue, going out as I thought to the spot where the rocks made imitation clouds, the dog along with her.

I felt lumpen, stranded, like the bit of moon and I thought with longing of the two of us down there, hand in hand, together, plumbing the deep, my coming to know and trust the water through her, growing free, like seaweed, or reed.

People came with their children, their dogs, their swimming paraphernalia, and soon the waiters were carrying plates piled with calamari and chips thin as matches. One little boy made everyone laugh, because on seeing the rock, down below, which had a huge hole through its centre, he asked if a giant had put his peepee through it. A beaded curtain divided the counter from the restaurant itself and every time the till was opened a little bell tinkled.

She came up the steps shouting with glee. She was mindless of the people around, as she called to me from afar, to look, look. She stood before me, dripping wet, her arms outstretched, proclaiming to have a blue body. Was she not blue throughout? The colours of the sea had got into her, the blue and the violet and the indigo had seeped into her like dye. They had. They had. She splayed her fingers, insisting on their blue surface and on the paler blue in the crevices. She was blue, upon blue, a creature Picasso had painted. Everyone stared, infected by her gaiety. It was as if she was determined to shock them.

'Do I look like a boy?' she asked.

'I don't know,' I said.

'Take a look at me and tell me ... someone, some young man, down there, thought I was a boy,' she said as she sat and opened the big wine menu which I had placed before her. The sun made little zigzags on her bare arm as she read aloud – 'This much-favoured wine comes from a region straddling the Gironde and the Dordogne, with strong British connections stemming from Henry II's marriage to Eleanor of Aquitaine.'

'We'll have that,' she said, and then asked the man if the gambas were caught that morning and how were they cooked and told him not to skimp with the garlic. First we would have spinach with cream and nutmeg. She was starving, ravenous. She jumped up and grabbed a basket of bread from the next table. She hadn't eaten since the day before – another drama in their house, their crazy house. A stranger had called, in the evening, a dark, swarthy fellow with eyes that rolled round and round, a fact that convinced her mother that he was a drug addict. She herself was not there, but of course in the inquest that followed she had been given every detail, the rolling eyes, his menace, the certainty that he must be on drugs. He had arrived uninvited, had knocked on the open door, and had said her name – 'I have come to see Catalina.'

Her mother went berserk and no wonder. Where was Catalina? No one knew. Her sister was already home from evening Mass but she had not seen any sign of Catalina there, Catalina had fled.

While she was telling me this, she put a present on the table for me, a gift from the sea, two beautiful stones perfectly rounded and looking so like biscuits that I almost put my teeth in them. One had a pale green coating like green icing and the other was like fudge. She took pride in telling the story of the stranger because this added to her sense of mischief, her longing for danger. Her mother, sister and father knew at once that because he said her name, because he said Catalina, he must have met her, and that she must have tantalized him to the extent that he came and searched her out. She laughed as she described the scene, her little nephew bursting into tears and calling the stranger the Devil. The stranger, it seems, sat there glowering, without being invited, his eyes going round and round but lingering quite often on the dish of warm paella that they were too frightened to eat. Each time her mother asked him what his business was, he blurted out, 'Catalina, Catalina.' Her sister swung her prayer-book before his eyes and told him that Catalina was not there, asked him to please leave, since they were farming people who got up at five and would now like to eat supper. He pretended not to understand. He said the name Franco which annoyed them further. The mother had to retreat to the bathroom a lot because his arrival had upset her stomach. The little boy cried and kept calling him Devil, Devil. When the mother switched on the television they learned the shocking news that there had been a rape in the vicinity that afternoon. Mother and sister at once came to the same morbid conclusion. Catalina had been raped. This man had raped her, because criminals always return to the scene of the crime. She laughed as she said this, laughed and ate ravenously. The gambas had come and she cracked the glazed shells with her teeth, then spit the shells out. The criminal had come to their house to expiate himself. Realizing this, her mother began to stagger, she always staggered when she was afraid. Her father, to show his importance, hit the plates with the big spoon and the little boy followed suit. What were they to do, the mother asked her husband, who merely shrugged and said he did not know since he was not a woman and had never been raped and that anyhow, women were the stupidest creatures on God's earth. He had no intention of attacking the stranger or defending the two women present if the stranger should strike again. It was up to mother and daughter. They repaired, it seems, to the back of the kitchen, where they hatched their plan. They offered him a repast. Rosario did it. She led him to the table, put him sitting with his back to the door. She ladled some paella on to a plate and begged him to eat. The two women then went to the well, filled a bucket of water, re-entered the dark kitchen, crossed stealthily, and struck at the stranger as he was diving in to the food. As they poured the water over him, they began to wail like witches and then the little boy joined in, helping them to drag the drenched victim across the kitchen, out the door, and down the path, where he could sleep under the stars, before he was found, as he would be, by the police. Once inside the house, the mother began to ring people to ask if they had seen Catalina or if they heard if she had been raped. She tells me all this, as if she herself had been there, party to every second of it. They pounce on her, converge on her as she arrives home, they maul her, thump her, question her about this man so that she has to admit that yes, she knew him, gave him a lift from the city, that morning on her way back from selling the lemons.

'In my van, in my van,' her sister screamed. Catalina, refusing to be cowed by them, had picked up the little boy who had fallen asleep, and gone to bed, hungry and surly. The stranger, as she said, was by now probably dying in a ditch from pneumonia. He had come from Wales, hoping to make a new life, to see a bit of sunshine, and what did he get but a douching.

Each time, before she lifted her wine glass, she dipped her fingers in the blue fingerbowl and once our fingers met in the cloudy, lukewarm water and I felt a current go through me, half fear, half desire, but when I looked at her she seemed oblivious.

'I often think of my mother and father when they were young ... so young ... so vital ... my mother, strong and well-built like me, in her black dress, her black shoes and stockings ... a migrant ... who had come from the other side of the island ... with the workers ... to pick olives ... my father seeing her ... deciding on her, flirting with her ... lifting his eyebrow the way you saw him lift it ... giving signals ... at lunch ... when they all sat down, winking ... making sure that she had the best piece of bread ... and in the evening when she lay down ... they all slept out of doors ... they all brought their own blankets ... my father going in search of her ... finding her ... bringing her somewhere very quiet and beautiful ... to his own house, maybe ... he owned the house and the land ... he was the master and she was the slave ... but he was the handsome master and she was the willing slave ...'

Then she told me that she was going to tell me something she had never told anybody in her life. I flinched in case it was something too intimate, while in another part of my being I longed to share all her secrets. She believed that she knew the exact moment when she was conceived, that she was there then, there for the gasp and for the magnitude of it but that she had not wanted to be conceived or to be born. The time was not ripe. I thought it a strange thing for one so young. This revelation came to her after she had taken some magic mushroom. She had taken it in another country, far from home, with someone else. She had seen visions, ravishing and frightening by turns. She had written them down and maybe one day she would show them to me, but then again maybe she would not. The man she was with wrote some of it, so that she was not certain which thoughts were hers and which were his. After lunch we sat and lolled, watched the people drift away, and the little mongrel dog, her errant escort, carry a bit of bamboo on to the terrace and wait for someone to throw it over the railing, allowing him to renew his mad canter.

The mountain was her bastion, the sea her passion and she marvelled at that surface that housed lions, calves, woods, flowers, fish; all subject to the most terrible transmutations. She loved the sea, she said, loved it in all its phases, she had lived, looking at it for over twenty years and it was still a mystery to her, she did not have eyes deep enough to take it in, in all its depths. No albatross she.

Upstairs in the ladies' room she had grown light-hearted again. As we stood in front of our respective mirrors, she lifted her white lace blouse, geisha-like and said, 'I cleared two terraces to get this blouse.' Her body was thin and wiry and for some reason made me think of a guitar. She had a little scar on her stomach, a zigzag knife cut. Music suddenly blared. With the luncheon guests gone and the head waiter off home to have his siesta, the other waiters allowed themselves a bit of levity as they cleaned the tables and quaffed what was left in the wine bottles. Suddenly and without deliberation she put her arms out, as if weaving through water, and then she started to dance, a lazy dance, moving not just to the music, but to some inner sway. Her fingers tapered and her shoulders went round and round with the ease of new tennis balls. She made me dance with her and carried away by her own boldness she led us out of the cloakroom into the long corridor with floor-length windows that opened to the garden. I felt certain that we were going to levitate while also fearing that I moved with the stiffness of an old perambulator.

'Let go ... let go,' she said in a whisper.

'I can't.'

'Of course you can ... first your feet ... then your knees ... then your head ...'

'I can't,' I said again. To make matters worse the waiters had formed a circle down below and were clapping to show their appreciation. I prayed for us to stop, but on and on she went, over the tiled slippery floor, getting adventurous in answer to their catcalls.

'They're watching,' I said.

'Let them watch,' she said and from time to time she made a face at one of them as if to challenge him. He shouted some name up and her reply was a shrug.

'What is he saying?'

'He's reminding me of my past,' she said and added that he was a cheeky fellow.

Later, and as a reward she said that I could come and milk
the goats with her. Normally her mother and the little boy
went, but for once her mother could sit at home and bathe
her poor feet. I waited on one of the terraces not far from
her house while she went off to get Carlos. It was a respite
to come away from the naked glare of the sea-light, to this
bower, the eyes soothed by one green after another, the dark
green of the flowering oaks, the silverish green of the olives,
the branches of pines like feather, forming a screen between
oneself and the world. It was as if I was being dreamed, as
I sat there waiting for her, the tips of the young pine trees
yellow-orange, votive candles ablaze in the golden afternoon
sun. I thought that perhaps my mind was made up, that
this surely was the place for me to stay, and moreover my
friendship with her was no longer so stilted. At some
moments the birds were singing and warbling and then again
a silence reigned as if they had all been whisked away to one
of the other terraces. I thought of poor Charlotte alone at
Ca'an Pintada, hiding and weeding, and I resolved that I
would write to her, ask her for a drink, make some little
overture now that I was happy. Some children passed, their
hair the colour of molasses in the sun and on the terrace just
above me a man was pulling a donkey on a rope and playing
with it, lasso-like as if he was at a rodeo. They came, chatting
like grown-ups. Carlos would say something and she would
repeat it, or exclaim as if he had said something preposterous.
He had obviously slept well because his face was smooth and
his hair newly brushed. He had a stick and with it he
thwacked everything that he passed, at times adding a hearty
admonishment. She didn't linger, she simply nodded to me
and I took up steps behind them. A feeling of delicacy
overcame me, a qualm as if I shouldn't be a party to their
chatter and moreover it set me off on another train of thought,
memories of my own children as children. I smelt them
there and then in the mountain air, a memory smell, quite
distinctive, as distinctive as bread smell or a gardenia. I could
see their little newborn wrestlers' bodies, being sprinkled
with dusting powder, the powder bluish in the crevices, and

how for years and years they adhered to me like limbs, branches growing out of me, wanting to do everything that I did, jumping into my high heels, or putting perfume behind their ears in imitation of me, and then the gradual stretching, burgeoning – chilling. Their spurts of independence, like choosing clothes that were in defiance of the slightly old-fashioned knitted things that I had togged them out in, then the motorcycles and the scenes that were the prelude to their departures. I thought that perhaps it was their child-hoodness, as much as his love, or my own long-vanished youth, that I mourned, or that they had all merged into one prism of sorrow.

'What is he talking to you about?' I asked.

'He says he loves me,' she said proudly and repeated all that he had been saying – 'I love you, I love carrots, I love nuts and I love the goats,' adding that it was a complete turn-about, because in the morning before she set out for lunch he said he hated her, that he hated carrots, that he loved chocolate, weapons, war and killing. He had gone around the house and into the yard using his stick as a gun, assaulting flowers, trees, chickens, anything, that got in his way. He was like that, full of moods. He would hide in a mud house with his imaginary friend, Giorgio, and they would plot terrible things – battles, raids, thefts – then in the evening he would relent and kiss her and go back to being an angel and ask for a fairy tale.

'Does he prefer you to his mother?' I asked.

'Sometimes,' she said.

The goats came down to meet us, their bleats ahead of them, three generations of goats, a kid goat, its mother and an old he-goat. They were off-white, with speckles, their tongues the colour of blueberries. She had brought a little corn in a pan to lure them, and their tongues ached to gorge on it. She said not to be duped by those soft tongues, they could eat anything, they could eat thorns, and did.

'Are you strong?' she asked.

'Why?' I said in reply.

'I want you to hold her, while I milk her,' she said and

placed my hands on the crown of the goat's head where I could feel the two stumps of wizened horn. The little boy was given the task of keeping the he-goat away. As she knelt she removed a cloth flap from the goat's teats – a precaution, because the other two would drink her dry. She had no illusions about family love whether it was among people or beasts. She held the bottle slantwise and the milk came in little dribs as the goat bucked and reared to try and escape and join her companions whom the little boy was supposed to be herding. He lost interest in his task as soon as a cat appeared. It was a huge fluffy white cat which kept watching the milk, like one mesmerized. At moments when the goat seemed about to break loose Catalina shouted, asking if I had never held an animal before. Determined to make the most of the journey she seized the second empty bottle and began to draw on the pink shrivelled teats. I held the tepid full bottle in one hand while with the other tried to keep some hold on the goat which grew more agitated as the last dregs were eked from her. Afterwards Catalina gave her a sort of embrace, as a reward, then retied the cloth flap, stood up and looked around as if she was seeing the place as a stranger might see it, as I might see it. All was silence, the olive trees with their gnarled roots and their distorted trunks seemed like figures in an enchanted slumber.

'I could live up here,' she said, 'with the goats and the grasshoppers . . . my own special little life . . . Carlos and me.'

'Why don't you?' I said.

'Because fairy tales are things to dream about,' she answered, quite abruptly, as if I ought to know that.

We stopped by a little house while Carlos fetched a plate, to pour milk for the cat. It was the tin plate that she had bought at the market. The house was only half finished and there were roof tiles and bags of cement lying about. It was called Ca'an Serra, 'House of the Mountains'. She had built it so far, dragged the stones and the cement up, in a wheelbarrow. One day she would live there, she and Carlos would live there, then she would be independent. The two sideposts and the lintel above the door were daubed with red. It was the blood of a ewe. Her grandmother had done it with a hyssop branch, to keep the evil one out: they believed in spells, in spirits, in incantation. They studied the flight of taloned birds and entrails for signs, signs in the colour of the gall and the symmetry of the liver lobe. Her grandmother had reared her, had told her many secrets and together they travelled back in time to their bivouac days, to their Moorish ancestors. They saw what mortal eyes could not see. 'People think we are mad,' she said, with triumph. The cat watched us walk away, watched with a sort of knowingness, then darted through a window space to guard the house.

Where the paths forked we said goodbye. She seemed downcast, grumbling that she must go to sleep early because she was getting up at five. I watched her walk away, a little sad, a little disgruntled and seeing the sag of her shoulders I thought of what she would look like when her children were grown, her body drooped from the toil and the years.

'I'll see you tomorrow,' I said. She turned and looked at me with a baleful look. The tears in her eyes were so big they seemed like glycerine drops.

'Why are you crying?'

'Because I'm so happy ... so happy,' she said but I could see that she was lying.

The letter was in my box the following morning along with the English-language newspaper. It was on ruled paper and written in capitals. It said,

SHE'LL DOE IT AND DOE IT AND DOE IT TILL DAWN.

(Robert Burns)

My body froze, as I looked about, thinking that maybe the anonymous sender was sitting in one of the armchairs watching my trepidation as I read. I was suddenly afraid. People disliked her, there was something in her that provoked malice, envy. I saw the many glances when we were together, the looks, the nudges, the innuendoes and I thought how foolish to forget that I was in a small place where nothing, no matter how harmless, went unseen.

Thirteen

The flowers lay on the table, inert, some secured with rubber bands, all waiting for her ministrations, except that she had not come. By noon there seemed to be a consensus that she was not coming. She had not even resorted to her customary ploy, which was to send her sister Rosario with a note to say she had been taken ill. Her apron and her flashlamp were also gone. Rumours abounded, such as that she had gone to the rival hotel, or that she had joined a circus and the burly hotel manager said that wherever she had fled to, it was in self-interest, because she never did anything that didn't suit herself. The girl with the moustache said she believed that she had gone to work for the lady who had stayed in the hotel and who had had to have milk with which to wash her face. This I assumed to be Iris. I felt downcast, miffed. I took to the street, paced, in the hope that I might hear news of her. Eventually I found myself going up to the church, entering, genuflecting, uttering childish prayers in a sing-song, distracted voice, that was devoid of devotion. Without the phalanx of accusing women I saw the various statues as fading and grotesque testaments to gore and suffering. The altar stripped of flowers looked bare and spartan, not at all the place for sacrament, or consecration.

Coming down the hill a girl stopped me. She had greyish skin, like putty, and long hair which was severely and unremittingly drawn back. I thought at first that it was to discuss something about the church, or to ask for money maybe, but

I soon saw the spleen in her expression. She asked if I realized that I was in a small village, a small community, where each person knew each other person, intimately. Her lips were thin and met tightly like the leaves of a prayerbook. Being English as she was, she brought to my mind those deserted country churches with damp weeping walls, unattended pews, a psalm on ravelled embroidery, lesson books, and hand-printed signs appealing for things for the fete. How often I had slunk into them to mutter some appeal for him.

'I am a visitor here,' I said, mustering authority.

'Visitors come here and try to taint the locals.'

'Do you mean Catalina?' I said boldly.

'I mean Catalina,' she said and in her eyes I saw an admission of love, buried, shocking – a love so intense, so intricate, she herself did not understand. I felt the colour rise in my cheeks, imagining that she saw into me, saw my own desire mirroring hers, wild, inchoate, covert; a desire without precedent. To calm myself, I kept running my fingers over my room key, smoothing the metal as if it was flesh, trying to forestall one of those cloying berserk battles, that I had always envisaged, with a woman, at least a certain kind of woman, the ones who issue strictures or commands, who have replaced the milk in their paps with something tart and sour, the harridans. I dreamed of slapping her face again and again, pounding her, disfiguring her so that she became grotesque, a laughing-stock to all who saw her.

'She is a free spirit,' I said.

'She is a respectable girl, from a respectable family,' she said and added that she and Catalina worked the land together, that their terraces adjoined, they went three evenings a week to water their crops, they worked like donkeys, they depended on each other. Her pride in telling me this was so great, so sensuous that I felt that if she were to give vent to the passions within her, she would swoon and lather like any medieval mystic. I thought of the several nuns who had taught me, nuns with the hushed footfalls who begrudged us our passage through the town each evening, where we could see street lights coming on, or clothes in shop windows, and although we could not linger, we could hear men and boys talking or whistling as they mounted their bicycles or walked their greyhounds.

'The land is her life ... not restaurants and scooters,' she said, coming closer to me, as if to strike me, or at least tug at the collar of my jacket.

'I think you have made some very rash assumptions,' I said.

'Not at all rash,' she said, getting the last word, because presently she turned on her heel and went down some steps to let herself into a basement house which I imagined to be hers. I wanted to run after her and continue the argument while at the same time I pitied her, grizzled as she was, with sorrow.

It had begun to rain, drops that did not get heavy, but fell sullenly, were eked from the sky. Because of the weather, the hotel lobby buzzed with people who sat and treated themselves to mid-morning tea and mid-morning coffee with slices of cake dense with cherries and green candied peel. Some kept pestering the girl behind the desk, asking her the price of the items of jewellery in the glass case. There were earrings, rings and bracelets laid on twigs or on stumps of semi-precious stone. I decided on a spree. I bought a pair of earrings that were symbols of fertility, rounded and wholesome, silver ovaries.

From the landing that approached my bedroom I could see a tiny portion of mountain through bars, six iron bars with seven oblong spaces, showing me a patch of mountain, trees clinging to a breast of rock. Was this my life, was this my vision, as limited, as petrified as this and through bars, from some unnamed prison. I thought of going back to search out the putty-faced woman, to violate her.

I thought of going to Catalina's house and warning her parents, I thought of confiding in one of the maids, except that I was not sure what it was that I wanted to say; in the end I rang the desk and told them that I would be leaving at the end of the week. By way of installing myself in my own house I rang my own number and hearing it ring and ring, I traipsed around the room and saw objects that had in themselves become witnesses to my life, and in one of those moments of muddle I included certain objects that were no longer there, that I had thrown into skips or rubbish dumps because they had become reliquaries of him. I saw not with the scales of memory but with palpability that overwhelmed me, that very first day when we had made love in my sitting room, a winter day, by the fire, on cushions, a bank of them, purple velvet cushions with gold lacings. There had been about it a detachment, a nonchalance, and I felt certain that I would not repeat it, or hunger for it. At the time it did not seem too important, did not seem like one of those brooches that, though pinned to the bosom, can sometimes accidentally go straight through to the flesh and the bone beneath.

Afterwards I went to prepare lunch and he made some attempt at restoring order to the room but he had done it so clumsily, in such an amateur way, that when I came back I laughed aloud, seeing the curtains only half drawn back, straggling on their brass rings and the purple cushions in an ungainly mound on the chaise longue, dumped, allowing anyone, even a simpleton, to guess at once what had gone on in that room, in the daylight with innocent snow falling outside. Seeing his shy pride in what he had done, filled me with a tenderness that was not dissimilar to the tenderness I had felt for my sons when they were still very young and would do something ridiculous such as buy hats to make themselves manly, or in the case of my elder son acquire a walking stick, claiming as he did to be suffering from water on the knee. Imperceptibly I had admitted him, a seam had opened and he had joined the others, the very few others, whose bloodstreams I imbibed –

> And your blood in torrents
> Art O'Leary;
> I did not wipe it off
> But drank it from my hands.

Allowing the phone to ring and ring I re-entered my own room, opened the shutters and looked out on my paved garden and the stone buddha with its inscrutable expression. It grieved me to think that I had hurt myself by parting with my props, the cushions, the chaise longue, my glass lamp with a coloured globe overlaid with segments of colour, like candied peel, and then it came to me in one of those dreadful little revelations that I had run away not because I loved him too much but because I feared I had not loved him enough, that I had not loved him in the selfless way in which as a child I had loved the saints and the martyrs and that maybe as a grown-up I did not know how to love at all. I was not capable of the sacrifice.

A few people sat around the pool with fawn towels over their shoulders, drinking hot chocolate that was exactly the colour of the towels. Lights were being fixed inside the pool and the sleepy waiter had been given the task of going down with screws and discs which he was to affix at various points along the walls. Being a novice, he succeeded each time in dropping what had been handed to him and was to be seen diving deep into the water, his feet straight up in the air, as he rummaged around for things. Afterwards, with a pleased sheepish smile he came up to announce to the engineer that he had found some, but not all. It took an inordinate amount of time for each lamp and each saucer-shaped reflector to be fitted so that the ladies and gentlemen kept complaining or consulting their watches and making sarcastic remarks. The engineer ignored them. From each large cardboard box he would take the equipment wrapped in plastic bubble-paper, and open it in a leisurely fashion, often disappear and return without ever once acknowledging their fret. Then he would fit the wires and the flexes to the lamps and place them on a little table while he went off on some other apparently vital mission. Meanwhile the young waiter sat on the edge of the pool in his wet trunks, shivering. They were very smart trunks and had the names of various resorts splashed all over them. They could not possibly have been his own. Eventually

he decided to treat himself to two of the hotel's fawn towels
and once secured inside this luxury tent, he assumed another
expression, a sort of aristocratic bafflement, and presently he
was smoking and calling to one of his companions to bring
him a cognac and a *café noir*. His daydream was not to
last. He was hastily stripped of his toga, and once again
despatched into the pool. People drifted off, telling each
other and themselves that since the day was destroyed they
might as well go for a drive or go to the glass factory or go
and look at churches or any damn thing.

Around lunch-time when I was called to the telephone I
knew for certain that it was Catalina. I could hear her even
before she spoke to me at all, hear her confess that she had
run away and was asking for my indulgence. I was certain
that she had eloped with some man and thought that when
we danced in the restaurant that perhaps his name was the
one shouted out. But it was Iris, asking me in the sweetest,
and most suppliant of voices if I would, oh if I would do her
the teeniest favour, saying as she asked that she knew it was
an imposition, and would I forgive her, please, *prego, por
favor*. She had ordered two lamps and the stupid artisan had
delivered them to the hotel instead of the finca. She couldn't
trust a taxi driver on his own, since her driveway was a cart-
track, so would I bring them, holding them in my arms
like the precious booty they were. She would give me tea,
cinnamon toast, maybe a little glass of champagne, she might
even find me a present, a trinket. By asking me I felt that she
had forgiven me for having listened to her tape; I felt vaguely
flattered, or at least relieved. Even before I said yes, she was
thanking me, saying she would pay the taxi of course and
give him a handsome tip. I could take him on to the port if
I wanted to, have a joyride. I was to guard the lamps with
my life. They were divine, simply divine, lapis lazuli, they
were for her *bijou* apartment in Rome.

A servant opened the door and I could see Iris coming
through the archway, hands out, to receive her trophies. She
wore a worried expression. The thing was, she tried to phone
me, but I had left. Plans had changed. She was leaving

straight away, we could not have a *tête-à-tête*. Her maid was
packing and naturally she must oversee it. She took some
money from her pocket and went out to pay the taxi driver.
Then a whim of decorum possessed her and she said I must
come up if only for a minute and have something, a glass of
Vichy perhaps. She put me in the little sitting room that led
to her bedroom as she hurried in to say something to whoever
was packing. She alternated between praising her one
minute, then showering her with abuse, then coming into
the anteroom to say some little pleasantry to me. She would
say my name, slowly and languorously, then ask if I was
having fun or if I had found a beau or if the hotel was still
full of shopkeepers, estate agents and anorexic upstarts from
Battersea. The maid appeared, weighed down with two
gigantic trunks. She was old and had unmatching brightly-
coloured shoelaces in her canvas shoes.

'Nobody packs like her,' Iris said, adding that it was a
miracle to get her at all, since everyone wanted her, booked
her weeks, even months ahead. She had a shawl draped over
either arm, one was black, embroidered with red and white
and the other turquoise, its flowers embroidered in the same
colour, except the calyxes had a silver glisten to them, like
thistles in frost.

'They would look so pretty on you,' she said, and she
allowed me to touch them, to feel the threaded pistils, and
the little central nodules that someone had so devotedly
stitched. Then she hurried back into the room and exclaimed
because the señora had done something awful, something
unheard of. Words passed between them and soon it was
apparent that the señora was not a slave who packed for the
rich but a virago in her own way, an artist who well knew
how to throw a tantrum, because she was coming through
the door obviously threatening to leave. Iris hauled her back
and from the pitch of the voices it was clear that they were
both old masters at it.

Iris appeared in tears. Imagine it, the cretin was putting
the lamps in, without wrapping them in anything, merely a
tablecloth. She hated to do this to me, but she just couldn't sit

with me because the moment she turned her back something disastrous happened.

'When I think what I pay her,' she said, waving a fist towards the door. The señora came out with some more cases, smaller than the first size. They were lizard and were of a mottled grey-blue; they emanated a sort of menace, stationed there waiting for their despatch. Somewhere in one of them, tucked perhaps in a scarf or a pillowslip was the tape, the smothered secret. I rose to go.

'When will you be coming to Paris?' she asked and managed a girlish pout when I said that I did not know. I could hear a car turning in the front driveway and the dogs and peacocks resuming their frenzied cries. To my surprise, I saw D'Arcy get out of a sports car. He was in a white suit and boater and instantly put his finger to his lips to ask for my discretion. He did not know me. Iris rushed towards him, all composure and hauteur gone and said, 'You came, you came ... my beautiful Lochinvar,' and the last I heard was D'Arcy spouting about white Ophelia ... her dreaming brow ... her golden hair, as he spun an excited Iris round and round, while she begged to be put in her chariot, with her Pharaoh.

Fourteen

First it blew and then it snew
Then it friz and then it flew
Then it friz again.

It was only a few days later that I looked up from my deck-chair to find D'Arcy, raw, unshaven and full of animated bile. He managed a smile however as he put his hand out and said meekly, 'The poor you have always with you.' He was still dressed in the white suit but had discarded the boater.

'Situation dire ... need shekels nunc,' he said, calling at the same time for a drink to lubricate his scalding brain. As we went across to the bar he held my arm protectively, as a suitor would and bowed to everyone that we met. At the counter however he erupted when the barman proceeded to pour his lager into a glass. Did the oaf not know, not recall that Ignatius D'Arcy abhorred and eschewed other people's pusillanimous germs. The barman put the bottle on the counter and turned away to write the amount on my bill. D'Arcy drank quickly, pronouncing it a good gargle, a salve to the nightmare. His frolic with Iris was over, abruptly terminated as he said, adding that Venus and Cupid had had some very rum jokes at his expense. He even apologized for the ungallant fact that he had snubbed me in her driveway.

'I seek neither truth nor likelihood,' he said, 'but I seek astonishment, as the blind Argentinian has said, and I tell you brother, sister, there was no astonishment. If she had left me alone, it might have been all right, it might have been, "Awake, Iris, thou first amongst women" ... libations pumped into her ... but as it was, it was a question of suspension of all animal strength ... desire vamoosed, nay knackered.'

He asked very gently, very solicitously if by any chance we could sit down and if he, D'Arcy, who had not eaten could be permitted to suffer the enticements of an Armagnac. He carried the bottle across to one of the tables and pulled the chair out, ceremoniously allowing me to sit down. I thought, we will squander the money that he so badly needs, but I was too nervous to thwart him.

'Where is she?' I asked, dreading a swish of skirts on the steps, for Iris's umbrage I knew to be considerable.

'God forbid it ... quoth he,' he said and looked about sharply to make sure that nobody could overhear us.

'Kept me prisoner she did, we were in this gigantic suite – numero 1503 and 1504, as I recall it; matching dressing gowns, little chocolados on the pillow ... "Isn't it cosy?" she said ... Cosy ... cosy ... Jesus ... of all the words in the vernac I abhor it most ... it and sincere ... a maggot is sincere ... we have just stepped into the room and she bids me to perform ... the Stud ... little knowing that I have surrendered all intentions of same. As far as I am concerned it is going to be bar-hopping and discoteca but no intergalactic sex on chocolada pillows ... piece of meat in permanent purdah ...'

He hit his forehead and asked himself in the name of Euclid and Pythagoras how he had got embroiled at all. A sort of rueful smile lit his features as he recalled their first entanglement – and spoke as if to himself – 'She tried all the winsome, wonsome ways the four winds had taught her ... She tossed her stumastelliacinous hair like the Duchess of Alba in her light gown spun of Sistine shimmer ... half strumpet, half milk-maid.'

Soon buoyed with drink and careless of those who passed by, he bawled out every detail of their rendezvous and his own sorry part in it.

'But you must have liked her ... you eloped,' I said.

'For a brief and shining moment I saw her otherwise ... glimpsed the magic gnaw in her eyes ... devilishly flattering light, plus devilishly flattering see-through gown, sharp-toothed necklace, jewels everywhere; blue, sapphire, amethyst ... over at her finca it was ... candlelight, chicken au poivre, venerable wines, telephone calls from far-flung resorts and I thought this is it, D'Arcy...' and he knelt as he re-enacted the proposal and called for slow music please.

Then he sat down, drank some more, shed some tears and as if talking to himself relived every moment of the proposal and the theatricality of it – 'I get off my chair, I get down on one knee, and lunatic that I am I beg for her hand. That was exactly eleven days ago. I need hardly say that she accepts, jumps up and down like a yo-yo, does a few pirouettes, Nijinsky style and says, "You naughty man, you naughty man making a fool of an old woman like me." I confess to undying love. We make a plan, a lifetime of plans, Cleo and Marc Antony on their barge, the world opening up before us, the Nile, the mouth of the Nile, the source of the goddamn Nile and meanwhile in some small crevice of the cranium a thought is being deposited that I will give her a year, perhaps two and then I am a free man, a man of means, that I will set out for Japan and track down that wench, one Ming who has lascivious powers over me and I will even know if D'Arcy the spoilt priest has spawned an offspring or not ... she asks if it can be a plain gold wedding band, nothing too ornate, something simple and chaste to match the sagacity of our years. She sees us walking under lime walks in our extreme old age. She omits to note that her old age has a decade on mine. I might have sniffed something fishy ... a rich woman, alone in a finca with no friend, no husband, neither kith nor kin but she fooled me ... asked me not to trifle with her. She even demurred. She begged if she could think about it, said she had accepted too blithely, asked if she could give it the vigil of a night, and Jesus I fell for it. We were alone, two storm-tossed seagulls or barnacles or some other migratories ... We could be a team, a team together, buffeting the winds.

Crafty, the common touch. Buddies. Not man and woman but Team. I did not lay a finger on her ... I did not go up the twelfth-century staircase ... She waved to me from the gallery ... blew kisses, trilling kisses, a suite of kisses, flourished an embroidered shawl ... 'tis but a spring to catch an impecunious cock like me as Jolls Joyce has already sagely noted. I came home. Pondered. Succumbed. Gave up my studio, Jesus, gave up my studio, and not long after, in fact two matins later, you saw me in her driveway, in white suit and boater, relics from my dandified days, and as you know we set out with an army of luggage, enough to go up the Nile or to pitch a tent in the Sahara Desert. First stop, Barcelona and I tell you it was not "Yon Dumo San Colon", but hosiers, seamstresses, furriers, jewellers and crimpers ... it was yours truly in tow, as Iris tried on one gown after another in some midget-size boutique. Iris caparisoned in purple, in gold, in turquoise and in eau-de-Nil. Then it was back to the boudoir for the grand toilette and our first bathe together ... Up to the big suite in the deadly silentest of lifts ... down a glittering corridor ... she plonks the "No Disturbar" sign on the door and claws at my starched shirt in her haste to remove it. Jesus, I'd rather be taken with an apoplexy like Gustave Flaubert or suffer the blind piles like the Irish friars than go through that fiasco again. She undresses to show a good example. Her waist and her thereabouts, white as lard ... never saw sunlight or even lamplight ... Acting like a little plebeian ... saying things ... Endearments. I cannot stand endearments, words like sweet or sweetie-pie. I cannot stand the oils or perfumes she has lathered herself with, and I cannot stand those thin white arms barnacled in bracelets, but oh the voice, the voice is the worst ... like gunge. Presently stump goes into sulkato. She bids it to rise ... to be gallant ... to show its prowess ... Marc Antony and Cleo tousling. It declines, visibly shrinks from her sight, like a retard. In my thigh energy not only a serious depletion but revulsion, puke. She begs me to allow her to do a little coaxing, a little somethinging ... I consider strangling her, but think better of it, and ask to be excused, to be allowed out, to stand on the terrace, to breathe refreshing fresh air, to which she says, "But of course . . . but of course," changing from Cleopatra muse to Florence Nightingale nanny, even dare I say it fashioning two pretty little poxy tears. On the terrace I see the harbour, I see ships in the harbour and express the wish to be the lowliest cabin boy, signing on. She has put music on . . . Edith Piaf . . . I listen to the Paris Linnet while addressing the shrivelled member and wait. The appellate decides to ignore me. Case clear. Phallus Banjax. She cannot wait . . . she puts her hand out, draws me in while in her other hand I see Vaseline. Title of reaction – Disgust. The Roman version.

"'Oh you little Roger, you little Scamp," she says, applying this unction, under the impression, false impression that her solicitude is going to incite me, member and all. Murder crosses my mind once again, only this time more strenuously. I think I will crush her with a pillow. I will do same without any of Othello's oscillations. When she sees that I am beginning to flip, evidenced by an open mouth poised for curse and imprecation she has the presence of mind to ask if there is something wrong? "Something wrong? Darling . . . darling?" she asks. "Nothing wrong," I say. I tell you I would not live those moments again for all the money and bishops' palaces in Feens, Swords, Limavaddy or Termenfechin . . . Old Edith choking away on the arrows of love while yours truly announces that he must have champagne and that it must be Cristal.

"'But of course, but of course," nursey says. While waiting for it to be sent up, she gives me the pukes by telling me that she understands, she quite understands, she mentions lovers in several continents, earls, counts, Knights of the Garter, all laid low with prostate, hernia or some other hardy affliction. For some reason that I will never understand I tell her a story that could only be calculated to offend. I tell her that Sir Isaac Newton was so absent-minded, that once and only once, when he loved a young woman, he sat smoking, silently, then at length, took his pipe and seized her hand, and she, expecting that he was about to kiss her, got the shock of her life when he stirred and cleaned his pipe with her little dainty forefinger. Jesus, she was up, clawing, screaming, Lady Macbeth instantato ... was it a young girl I sought ... was that it ... was I one of those middle-aged men who needed a young girl to stroke his ego ... if so, why had I led her this far, because after all we had both embarked on this, we had signed the contract. Contract! I was under house arrest.' He re-enacted the arrival of the champagne, a scut of a waiter, black trousers too tight, like a ballet fopper, tearing the dun-gold paper cork, holding the bottle with a pink napkin and opening it quietly and with conceit, then waiting for the emolument which she was loath to give. In the end she gave a pittance.

'Do let's talk,' she had said, as soon as the waiter went out of the room.

'I cannot speak more plainly,' was what he had said and to prove it opened the cord of the chenille robe which he had knotted before the flunkey came in. He roared with a mixture of rage and shame as he recalled her expression, her alarm which grew so great that she wondered aloud if she should call the manager and ask him to send up the hotel doctor; and putting her hand to it and not finding a fraction of elasticity she jumped and said he would have to do something, he would simply have to do something, as this was not good enough. Yes, she would call the doctor, he could get an injection of some kind, she was not putting up with this, this ignominy, she who had danced with the crowned heads of Europe, she who could be in Monte Carlo at that very moment, being toasted lavishly.

'Thunder and sparables,' D'Arcy said, reliving his ire. 'I mean there is nothing wrong with me, that a young girl or a young woman could not cure ... I find a young girl pulling turnips and I'm around her with my tricoloured equipment ... but not Dame Iris ... Oh no ... Dame Iris, now pet-itioning if she should sit on my lap, if that is it, if maybe I am just a teeny weeny bit kinky, if she could entice me therewith; and while staying my rage I do some serious thinking ... I think poison is the last resort of a Hannibal ...

The dagger the last resort of a Cato ... Incision of the veins the work of a Seneca ... but to this lapsed Christian poxy, silence, exile and cunning. So I tell her I must take a walk ... I am the brooding type ... if I walk along the harbour I will become myself again, my fundament restored to me. She deliberates. She agrees. I go to the dressing room and put on my white suit and my boater. I am now able to hum a little ditty. I come out smiling. She slips her hand into my inside pocket and relieves me of my wallet in which there lurked a few mangy dollars that I had oggled out of her to toss to menials. "I'll hold on to this," the cow said, reiterating her suspicion that I will go to a bar in search of eighteen-year-olds. On my exit she wags a dragon fingernail and tells me to hurry ... to come back under the hour so that we can dine and then boogie-woogie. Eighteen-year-olds! I haven't a fluke. I walk out of there penniless. I do not trust myself to use the lift lest she should follow ... I take a back stairs littered with banana skins and muck ... I am broke, hungry, humiliated but I tell you I feel like Clint Eastwood at the moment in Dirty Harry when he throws his police badge into the river.'

I used the moment to ask him how much money he needed to borrow. I dreaded that it would be more than I could afford. The light had faded, and the first star, that never failing emissary had appeared in the shallow font between the two ridges of mountain. Also by his shuffling I knew that the barman was waiting to close the outdoor bar in order to go down and work inside.

'Anything ... ten dollars ... twenty ... fifty ... even a hundred,' he said, putting his face in his hands to hide his shame.

'I bought some earrings here ... I can return them ... they were two hundred ...'

'No readies,' he said, or rather muttered.

'I'll see,' I said and hurried off, not in the least worried that I would have to part with the earrings, or put the refund towards my bill.

In my room I signed his name on two of my travellers

cheques, coloured cheques with lilac tints in them. They seemed to be more like paintings than money. When I got back to the terrace the bar was closed, the metal grating down, and no sign of D'Arcy. I thought maybe that he had gone across to the pool to have a stroll and I called expecting to see his figure, but all I saw was the restless sheet of dark water, and the poplars as always, sentient, keeping guard. I called his name a few times, and then as I went down the steps to search for him in the lobby, a young waiter came running towards me and handed me a note. I read it by the light of one of the lanterns. It said:

> Only friend ... not a word of truth in anything I said
> ... All for your amusement ...
> Con amor por amores ...

'Oh, D'Arcy,' I said aloud and to no one. The waiter was already disappearing, his white shirt in the dark, like a flying banner as he hurried to his next charge.

Fifteen

I found Catalina on the top step of the stone stairs that led
to my room. Her head was down and her hair spilt over her
face, covering it completely. At first, I was not even certain
if it was she, then I recognized her by her pink running shoes
and she looked up, desolated, haggard.

'I'm back,' she said lamely, admitting the mistake she had
made. She hated the city, had to share a room, an attic room,
with her friend Teresa who lived like a mouse. Teresa's little
girl, Aurora, laid low with whooping cough, barked all night.
She came to see me first to gather courage because she was
afraid to go home. She would be punished for weeks and
weeks. Then she ranted on about family ties, family chains,
family madness. Baby birds, she had read, never build a nest
within ten miles of the parent birds and she could see why.
Equally she should not have gone, she had made a fool of
herself.

'In what way?' I asked.

'There's only one way,' she said and nodded. Yes, it was
a man, and she threw herself at him; he was someone she
had met the previous summer at an English language course,
and she who believed that she would never fall in love again,
had fallen.

He was cold and austere but the coldness was only a mask.
She sensed that the first time she had set eyes on him, on his
sad, El Greco eyes and his long beautiful El Greco face. They
were staying in the same guest-house and on the last night

they all drank, students and teachers together and afterwards when she went to her room she couldn't sleep, because she knew that he was waiting for her, and on impulse she pulled a coat over her shoulders and went across to the main building where he was sleeping. She knocked on his door, surprised him, told him that she knew it was rash but could they talk, could they talk. He got dressed while she waited in the hallway and then together they went down into a big old rustling garden that lay above the sea and between the sighs of the sea and the rustle of the bamboo they talked, talked about everything, love, marriage, children. He confessed to her that he had dreamt of her on each of the three nights since they had met. Next day, being their last day, they walked in the garden again and she gave him a black pod full of black seeds and he told her that he had never told anyone the things he was telling her. He told her that he loved his country yet longed to leave it, that he liked teaching, yet dreamed of being free, far out at sea, alone, that he loved his wife and children but they were ropes around his neck, that marriage was a jail and life itself nothing but a purgatory. For a year she had thought of him and twice she had written and then one night, one fevered night, she telephoned him, wakened him, and he had said yes that he was happy to hear from her and that he would be happy to see her. Thinking it meant more than it did she gave up her job, lied to her parents, said that Teresa and herself were going to run a boutique in the city and even left the little boy.

'I hate myself,' she said and lamented the misery she had caused, then regretted losing her job and as she looked around she remarked that the flowers in my room were not profuse enough.

'Maybe they'll have you back,' I said.

'They won't ... they hate me ... they think I'm reckless ... just like he does.' Thinking of him afresh she burst into tears, recalled going to his rooms, in the university, finding the door open and waiting for him in his office, his coming in, his surprise at seeing her, his attempt to brush her off by looking about for books and papers, his postponing the

moment before he kissed her and then doing it so suddenly
that their noses collided and they drew apart shocked by the
current between them. Soon after, terse things were said.
She should not have come. Yes he remembered the garden
and the night they had spent talking, a coat thrown over
them, yes he remembered the black seed pod and yes he had
lost it or thrown it away, he was a different man now. Up
there in the north, he had forgotten his responsibilities,
reneged on his true feelings, he had been another man.
Nothing she said would make him admit either to the sweet-
ness or the shiver of what passed between them. He was
telling her to come to her senses, to study, not to waste her
life as he did, as so many did; to waken at forty or fifty to
find that they had missed the boat. Finally she asked him
one favour, one small favour and innocently, or else to get
rid of her, before his secretary came, he said yes. She asked
him to give her a baby. He looked at her as if she was
possessed. She went down on her knees and begged for him
and here she began to cry, repeating her words, her shameless
beseeching, his voice as he said, 'I can't give you a child . . .
I can't . . . I cannot . . . it would be milk . . .' thereby telling
her that he had had the sterilization that he had threatened
the night in the garden, that he had actually gone and done
it.

'Why would you want a baby?' I said, aghast.

'Because I want him.'

The movement of her lips, rapid, uncontrollable, told me
that if she were to speak she would break down completely,
she would own up to a sorrow greater than any she had
known before. I longed to be able to tell her something that
was not true, such as that it would be all right, or that he
would change his mind, or that she would get her job back,
anything to console her. From her bag she took a little
miniature rocking horse that she had got in a junk shop. It
was painted red and white, and there was glue on the face,
where a beard had been. It was for the little boy. He too
might not forgive her for a week. It was growing dark outside,
slanting pillars of darkness filling the courtyard, swoops of

it invading the room and far below those crêpe shivers, settling over the sea, presaging the cold at the oncome of night. There was nothing to be said. Each time she touched it, the horse sidled back and forth on its frame, giving a strange animal-like mewl and now that it was dark she allowed her tears to fall and asked all the whys, why she had not met him years ago, before he married, why he had given her to believe that there was something between them, why he was afraid of her, why, why, why.

Sixteen

'We'll be up there, far up,' she would say, making me queasy as I looked through the window of the bus at the jagged summits and the dizzying tree-clad slopes. Ranges of mountain appeared before us in a broken sequence as the bus furrowed its way over the narrow winding road. At times we had to stop to give way to another vehicle, but the driver, accustomed to such inconvenience, was cheerful and gave way to everyone. She had quarrelled with her sister, quarrelled with her parents; ever since she got back they were all surly with her, terrified no doubt that she would go again. Even the little boy refused to speak to her, called her a devil and would no longer sleep in her bed at night. Her sister refused to loan her the van because it was Sunday and she was seeing a friend.

'Friend!' Catalina exclaimed, and then, looking down at my green espadrilles, her anger spiralled. Did I think I was going to climb a mountain in those things?

'They're flat,' I said.

'It's steep ... it's rocky ... it's full of thorns and bristles ... it's a mountain ... you have heard of such a thing,' she said, giving the people around us the benefit of her invective.

'We needn't go,' I said, feebly.

'No, we needn't go,' she said and decided to devote her attention to a little dog on a leash who was eagerly trying to break away from its owner. I looked through the window at the road, bits of wall, and the sea down below still grey, a grey shimmerless net. I feared the mountain. Something told me I would fall or disgrace myself, or that we might quarrel. She was scowling, eyebrows puckered, and I could easily see why her little nephew called her a devil. I could barely trace in her scowl the memory of the girl who had put flowers in my room or had danced with me languidly.

In the town, we got off the bus in silence, and still smarting, I followed her foolishly up the street. Behind us an English group were planning their day and it was lamentably clear that the younger couple wanted to go off alone while the older couple did everything to cling to them. Eventually, when it was confirmed that the young couple were going to take a steam train to the city, the others capitulated, and the woman, making the best of it, said, 'On your camels then . . . on your camels.' Catalina could not resist a smile, a sort of sad smile, as the woman, to hide her disappointment, spoke formally and to no one, of the beauty of the place, and then addressed some chummy chastisements to a stray dog who was slinking in near the wall. I still felt it was unnecessary to buy walking shoes, since I had a pair in my cupboard at home. I could see them for a moment, all those shoes, cleaved and cluttered together, a jumble of black suede, brown suede, with straps of gold and silver and my thick, ungainly walking shoes, with padded insoles, shoes I had bought in America in order to be able to walk along the Atlantic coast and pick stones and think about him, as if thinking about him would induce him from afar to think about me. In the shop, she knelt and tied the laces of my new shoes, making big bows because of the laces being far too long.

'I'll have to take a photograph of you in these,' she said, trying to humour me. She had brought her sister's camera but there were only two shots left on the film.

Next door to the shoe shop was a cake shop, and it being Sunday, the confectioners were prodigal. There were wide pale buns, like hollowed breasts into which cream and custard had been poured. The cream was whipped and looked substantial whereas the custards were softer and spilt over. On a revolving, three-tiered glass cake plate there were little cakes dusted with castor sugar, their upturned alert wings like cats' ears, agog. There were tarts of every kind, some filled with jam, red and dark purple; others with an amber filling like opaque honey, all of them latticed with pastry. The smell floated out. It was both sweet and airy and cloying, and reminded me of the magic that I had invested cakes with, as a child, one in particular, an orange cake that seemed like a moist full moon. Catalina ran in, waving her cloth bag to show that she was going to buy something. On a cake tray, covered with waxed paper, was the local cake, yellow, made with almonds and egg whites and spread with lemon curd. She bought two slices, each one resting on its own sheet of waxed paper and assured me that it was not fattening. I bought another cake which had many leaves filled with purees of jam, which she predicted would melt, on the mountain.

'What is it like?' I said.

'It's like Mars,' she said, 'it's rusty, like Mars.'

Going down the street we ate the slices of almond cake. One of the waiters from the hotel shot by, tall and proud on a new scooter as if it were a steer.

'Where did you steal it?' she called after him and he turned and grinned, pleased to have made her jealous.

We looked in the various windows as there was time before the next bus. All the cups and saucers were bordered with deep blue, the blue I came to regard as being the colour of that place and of her – wild, vivid, cobalt. Beside them were glass ornaments of animals, absurd and funny, with twigs of glass like whiskers sprouting out of their noses and their mouths. There were the pots in every shade, the wide amphora pots, some brown as if they had just been lifted out of wet, boggy earth, others painted in blue or green and frosted on the inside, as if sprinkled with saltpetre.

We nearly missed the second bus and when she heard it and saw it approaching the monument, she ran, shouting, 'Pare, pare.' I ran after her thinking how the cake was getting squashed and half hoping we might miss it, so that instead we could sit in the square and have tiny cups of bitter coffee, then at lunch-time have grilled gambas and wine, and later rest in the shade under one of the big trees, where the people sat, talking and fanning themselves,

We drove along an exceedingly narrow road with houses and orchards on either side. The orchards overlapped, to form an endless canopy, light filtering through the leaves giving a calm and muted quality to everything as if the world itself were one vast dappled orchard. It was like being in a cradle, or a horse and cart, jogging along, our shoulders touching, our eyes soothed by the greenness that was enriched by the tinted window of the bus. She had pinned her hair up with two unmatching combs, one white and one diamanté, out of which some of the specks of glitter had fallen. Every so often she took a tube of cocoa-coloured ointment from her pocket, unwound the screw, moistened her lips and offered me some as if it was a lozenge or a cigarette. She was asking me what I had on my dressing table at home, if I had round pink bowls for powder and perfume sprays with crocheted nozzles and velvet flowers and caskets of jewellery. She had seen such things when she worked for ladies, visiting ladies or when she had given them massage.

'You do that too?'

'I have to do everything,' she said haughtily.

I described my room, a big bed, an old mirror, and cream wallpaper with garlands of rosebuds teetering on thin gold threading; a bow window that opened on to a garden where an owl nested in the old fig tree and kept me company at night by hooting softly, a lullaby. Why was I not there now, why was I in flight? What malady possessed me? I thought of a strange custom of my childhood which had to do with warts. To be rid of them we rubbed them with stones, then put the stones in a bag at an appointed place, for the fairies to take. Surprisingly the spell worked and the warts did go. I had been chasing from place to place to bury some affliction, to leave it somewhere except that no fairies came to the rescue and it dogged my every journey. At least now I was preparing to go back.

'Maybe you will come one day,' I said. She looked rueful and said that she doubted she would travel again, it always brought nothing but trouble. She was destined to be a drudge on the farm. She painted a heady picture of her decline.

Getting off the bus she took a folding timetable from her pocket and confirmed the time of the last bus with the driver. He seemed to know her or else it was that he was attracted to her because they shared some joke which I did not understand. Over one shoulder she carried a cloth bag in which she had everything for safari – bread, cheese, salami, olives, a bottle of well-water and the family wine. I hid my espadrilles at the side of the road, under some scorched grass and we had a bet as to whether they would be there or not when we returned. The tinted window and the drive through the orange groves had been misleading, the sun was boiling and streamed down as if from a molten funnel; it grazed and pierced the eyes; it leapt off the specks on her hair-slide and seemed to assault the cake through the white box with the absurd cerise ribbon. I felt as if I was being consigned to some oven, like white dough about to harden and bake. I wanted to turn back but cowardice and reticence drove me on. We took a path that zigzagged between the spindly trees and bushes and I envied the lizards hidden in the thorny brake. She took a squashed straw hat from her bag, laid it on my head and debated whether she should use up the film then or later.

'Later,' I said, every nerve in my body raw, rebellious.

The path was overgrown with scrub and thorn but underfoot it felt sandy with here and there bits of loose pebble and shards of rock. We passed empty houses, then one where dogs that were chained did everything with their snarls and their muzzles to get to us. She knew their names, she seemed to know the owners of all the houses, had worked for them or done piecework from time to time, such as digging their gardens or clearing their terraces. She moved like a goat or a young colt, darting from one boulder to the next. Some of the boulders were intact but others, torn in two by storm or lightning, had seared orange centres. Now and then she would pat an olive tree as she might a friend. The olive was her favourite because of the way it lived and survived in aridity. The oaks of course were not your English oaks, they were the runt of the species, but nevertheless they provided acorns for the pigs, charcoal for the fires, tannin for the hides and shelter for the shepherds and the charcoal-burners in times gone by. The world down below already appeared far away, the cars moving like toy cars at an ordained speed and the steeple of the church was a long needle growing invisible in the glare of pure light. There were flowers, single flowers, mostly blue and pale purple and once a butterfly flitted by and she ran after it, with cupped hands, to catch it in order to be introduced to me. Pointing to the oaks she said that the young boys and young men used to catch the thrushes, wait for them as they hurried home at dusk and catch them in their big nets, but that they would not do it again, because since Chernobyl the thrushes of the world had been contaminated and hoteliers would no longer buy them as delicacies for the guests. She said in its way it was a good thing that the tragedy happened, it made people realize that the world was one planet, countries were not separate, as they thought they were, but vast families joined by something far more important than creed, or politics, joined by nature; and answerable to one another.

We came on a little ruin that was covered with wild grass and brushwood. A few gangly blue flowers stuck out of the roof and seeing it in the near wilderness it looked like a fairy fort. She ran inside and called me, excitedly. It was almost dark except for the points of light through the holes in the roof; in one corner there was a bed made of grass and leaves and beside it a stump of red Christmas candle, half-burnt.

'Home,' she said with a flourish, designating the place as our cave with gongs, tapestries on the wall, deer being roasted, skins on the beds, us women and children huddled together as our knights rode off to war. She had read part of a book about things like that once. She had liked it but in the end found that it was too fantastic. 'So you do read...' I said, remembering how she had once chided me for sinking myself into my books. She said yes, that she liked fabulous tales about gods and goddesses and that her heroine was

Gaia, the earth mother who even when she lost everything, was not vanquished. It was the only reference to her recent and doomed escapade.

Outside I faltered at the sight of the steep bluffs, stone and still more stone, obelisks of boiling ochre, and the summit far up, too far.

'Why are we doing this?' I asked.

'I'll show you,' she said and she pushed me forward with prodigal strength. Soon I forgot the heat, all of my mind geared towards the danger. I felt powerless to go on yet equally powerless to go back. At times the sheer rocks were almost perpendicular and we had to scramble on all fours. When we came to a ledge that was a mere rim, overhanging a ravine, she said not to look, to just hold on to her. I stared straight ahead at a circular peace sign that had been stitched in black on the back of her T-shirt. Very slowly we went across and when we had made it, I saw that she too was trembling. There was sweat on her upper lip and she put my hand to her heart, to feel its agitation. It was beating fearfully, like a bird trying to break its way through a window.

After that, we came to an olive grove, the trees clinging together, holding each other up, like bowed witches. There was a ruin, some columns and a beautiful archway, a summer abode which an asthmatic king had built for himself. 'Cadira del Rei . . . the Walk of the Kings,' she said, as she strutted on. The worst was over. The last bit of the climb was a sheep track and far less daunting. It was odd and comforting to see the sheep scattering before us, thin sheep, scattering deftly, more like fawns, not bleating as if they'd taken a vow of silence. I felt elated, reckless. The first thing she did when we got to the top of the mountain – itself a fairly inauspicious sight – was to let out a holler, to inform the world that we had conquered. Then she took out the water bottle and we drank from it in turn and with gusto. She thrilled to be offering me a feast, her first as she said, and she would wink as she produced each thing – hard-boiled eggs, the salt already smeared on them, a chunk of cheese, very red salami that was thin and spindly, and little custards in tin cups. She poured the wine into other cups, added water and we drank ceremoniously to Beauty, to Risk, and to Mars. She produced her little knife and began to cut the bread and the salami. It was a Toledo knife. She had found it on a wall and had called it Fritz, after a character in *Swiss Family Robinson*. She apologized for not bringing a paella. Her mother's paella was the best in the world, tender, their own rabbits and poultry. As she said it I recalled seeing them, in their dust baths, peppering on the day of the sirocco.

'Has she forgiven you for going away?' I asked.

'Half and half,' she said. Her mother didn't address her in the house but when they went to milk the goats, she said a few rough words and that signalled forgiveness. She lay on her stomach then and began to eat, her face full of animation, a red shawl over one shoulder and I thought that this was the picture of her I would carry away, her talking, eating, confiding. It was not the first time she'd left home. She had run away at eighteen, gone to Turkey, she'd had an adventure there, many adventures.

Once at sundown, or rather before sundown she'd left the little town to go into the hills. Some children from a gateway ran to greet her, her shorts and bathing suit a fascination compared with their older sisters and mother and grandmother who were swathed in scarfs and veils. The children had dragged her in. It was a sort of courtyard where the women sat, on one long form, knitting. Underneath their swathed rags they wore floral pantaloons. They thrilled to see her and posed while she took photographs of them. The children clambered over a big red motorcycle, a Jawa, with wide handlebars and headlights like the eyes of giant insects. Each time that she took a photograph, they insisted on giving her a present – flowers or single petals, pink and white and pale rose. Then they gave her a little bag of golden fruits.

When she was leaving, the father, who had joined the group, asked if she would like a ride on the Jawa and she had said yes. Instead of heading for the town where her companion waited, they went up into the hills, away from the sea and away from his ramshackle farm. It was rough road after rough road and then across a stone field, until at length on a huge promontory he stopped the bike and got off. She had to get off too. She sat on a stone and he came and sat next to her. He tickled her kneecap and said words in his own tongue. When she moved to another stone he followed. So it was, from stone to stone, with her trying to pretend that nothing untoward was going on, and above all trying not to offend him. He took the bag of fruits from the saddle, handed her one and with gesticulation begged her to eat. She kept pointing to the village and the sea, the cobalt sea down below where she wished to be. He pressed the fruits on her. He ate one himself. He put a stone on her throat so that it slid down inside her bathing suit. It was small and shiny like a brown bee. She could not show fear. She tried to show fret. She began to scrape the ground with a piece of flint, to write the one word, town. After an hour of this he attempted to put an arm around her. She curled up as small as a lizard. Eventually and in a big sulk he went back to his Jawa and with head down she followed. In the town he dropped her outside the church, said nothing in the way of a farewell and revved off. In the one shop cum tavern her friend was waiting and he slapped her in front of all the Turkish men and brought her home, to the house which they had rented. He wrapped her in huge carpets where she sweltered and choked for two days.

'He was a carpet dealer,' she said wrily.

'Was he the professor?'

'Of course not . . . the professor was the one who was going to save me . . . make me forget him.'

'Where is he now?'

She shrugged, said she hoped he was in jail and said it was my turn to tell of my travels, but that I could save it, since it was time for her siesta. Then she turned over and put the shawl over her face, like a cowl.

The world seemed to pause under a great silencing weight, every bit of stone motionless, the air suspended as if holding its breath in a silence so vast it seemed to produce thickets of silence. My travels did not have the daring or the adventure of hers. I saw parts of America, I saw television screens with pizzas being dragged across them, voices on the radio that said depression could be treated and in the next moment talked of floorshows, fine dining and a city dedicated to pleasure and fun. I remembered how in the evenings I would go to that corner of Central Park where the horses and carriages were, for a whiff of the homeland, byres, milk smells and the stirrings of birds about to roost in the big lonely trees. There would be people hurrying to the subway, barricades of moving people that seemed far less human than the horses, who emanated some little flourish, some little breath of humanity, the plumes of their breaths like chimney smoke, the carriage lamps red on one side, a dancing gold on the other, and then the hooves prancing as a pair of lovers was conveyed into the park; horses indifferent to the chaos and traffic all around them, piebald horses, black horses and my favourite the chestnuts, among the throngs, glistening, their haunches so solid, their breaths so fine, spiralling, and snug inside the carriages, a tartan rug or two, a spray of flowers, even a horseshoe and in all of it a memory of country roads, that though I could not return to I yearned for and I thought how hard it is to part with anything, even the things that hurt most, especially the things that hurt most.

When she wakened she said that she had been dreaming of the East. She and the little boy were walking in Gethsemane, the little boy eating melons, eating and eating the striped green skins and the soft lime-green pulp, then the seeds, devouring them so that his teeth turned into seeds and were no longer the little square sturdy white teeth with sharp points but yellow and flaky, crumbling in his mouth.

'My grandmother will have to translate that,' she said.

'Does she translate your dreams?' I asked.

'Yes ... it's always the same thing, that I'm going to make a very long beautiful journey but she doesn't say where...'

'Maybe she will translate mine,' I said. She said she doubted it. She said I would be lucky if I ever saw her grandmother, because she hid most of the day and only came out at night, at night she was often called to houses to comfort the dying, those timid ones who are afraid to go.

We were so early for our bus that she decided to use up the film. Nearby was a field, dense with poppies, dense, flowing, it was like a lake; a swaying redness, on and on; more and more, heaving like a quilt, or a sea, a hallucinatory couch to lie down on. After the mountain they seemed ravishing, tender. We climbed the gate and went in, walking first along the edge, then halfway down a path appeared between the rippling petals and on tiptoe we followed it, across to a tree. She set the timer, put the camera a distance from us, and then together we squatted on the grass, waiting for a click that was so silent we were not even sure if it happened. As we were waiting, we heard the bus and she jumped, careless now of the sea of poppies, trampling over them, hollering but even as she ran she saw the bus come, pass, swerve round a corner, and as she climbed over the gate she shouted after it.

We hailed the first car that came, but it passed, and the next two were full of passengers and the fourth stopped but the driver could only bring us part of the way.

'We can take a taxi then,' I said.

'Muchas gracias,' she said to the driver and then turned to me and beamed. We both thought the same thing, that the day was too enthralling to bring to an end and that possibly we would never spend another like it. Yes, yes, we would go back to our little cave and bivouac. Going back up she planned the menu. She threw in everything. Paupiettes de Saumon . . . Petit Tournedos de Boeuf Sauté Bourguignon . . . Swordfish . . . Gazpacho . . . Gambas and Langoustines . . . Bouillabaisse . . . Mélange de Soufflé et Sorbet Marie . . . Gourmandise and Café Splendide.

It was dark by the time we reached the cave and the sky was pelted with stars, stars so bright and so fervent it was as if they spoke, as if each little grain of glitter conveyed a meaning; a signal. Numerous as they were, each one seemed to reside in a languid space, so that in looking up at them the eyes themselves expanded and swam in the wideness of the sky, marvelling in the velvet darkness. She bustled about, first having to find the candle, then light it cautiously since she was using her only match. She pared the dry wick, begged it not to falter, not to fail. Soon as it had taken, and the flame became steady, she left me to gather grass and leaves for our bedding and wood for our fire.

'Our fire?' I said.

'Of course,' she said. 'How else were we going to roast our venison, our potatoes and chestnuts?'

I stood there looking at the little wan blaze from the candle as it skewed hither and thither, thinking what a bleak place it would be, without her, what a dungeon, but her presence gave it the glow and ritual of a palace. I felt elated, as if set down in some faraway universe.

She came back with grass, branches and an armful of wood, for the fire.

'Will your parents be cross?'

'No,' she said. 'They'll think that we went to a restaurant and I'll be home in the morning before they get up ... The first bus is at five ... anyhow my mother thinks that you are a very respectable lady.' There was a little glint of mischief in her eyes as she said this. What was she thinking? Did she know that I had moped day after day when she left, that I had waited for her to come up the stairs and tap on my door, that I was certain that she would ring me from some strange town, or some railway station, just to tell me where she was and that twice I had dreamt she was in an accident?

She knelt and prepared the fire, putting thin little twigs on first, then heavier ones crosswise, and then reaching for the candle and lighting the wood, before piling on any more. The sticks caught fire, expired, all went dark for a moment as she pleaded and prayed, then a little spurt of flame issued through, retreated, then by a miracle attached itself to a thin piece of wood, which fired a neighbouring piece and soon the sparks began to crackle and the flames made leaping shadows on the mortar wall.

We ate outside so that we could look at the stars. She knew several by name and her favourite was Sirius, the Dog-Star, the brightest fixed star in the sky. We had some bread and salami from lunch-time and there was of course the much derided cake. She opened the sides of the cakebox ceremoniously to form a tray and then she cut big oozing chunks with her knife, Fritz. It tasted synthetic, full of almond essence and mock cream and various jams but she pronounced it delicious. We ate slowly but we drank heartily, toasting each other in whatever language we could think of. She knew far more languages than I did and knew the swear words in all of them.

'*Yegiba ... Yegiba...*' was the swear word in Yugoslavia. She would only say them in foreign tongues, not her own.

'Red or white, madam?' she would ask, becoming more daring with each draught. She had worked in a restaurant for two years, boasted of all the dishes she had dropped, the octopuses she had retrieved from the floor, timbales of crème brulée she had eaten, scandals she had witnessed. One night in the restaurant, a young man had gone berserk, attacked his father with a knife because his father had flirted with his new girlfriend. The waiters took the father's side, since he was a very important man, convened on the son, grabbed him, put him in the water trough and ran the hose on him until he came to his senses, disgraced and shivering. Soon after he went to the asylum, driven by jealousy. Had she been jealous? Yes, often, but she knew how to deal with it, the same man that tied her up in the carpet, had made her jealous, again and again. They were in Madrid once, a whole party of them had gone to the flamenco. She had brought her friend Carmen. Carmen was pretty and knew it. Carmen had a long back which she made sure everyone saw, because she wore low-cut dresses. She made her own dresses, copied the designs from ones she saw in grand shops. The moment he laid eyes on Carmen he was smitten. She knew it by the way he looked at her, by the way he asked her what she wanted to drink, by the way his hands shook when he poured the wine, then all through the dancing, he kept looking to see if she was enjoying herself or if she was bored or if she needed a cushion or another drink. At the interval he made a right fool of himself, ran out into the street and bought roses for all the girls, expensive bunches of red roses, spent everything they had. That night in bed she tackled him. He said yes, he loved Carmen, but only from afar, he worshipped her but he was not worthy of her, not worthy to tie her shoe.

She asked him what he loved about her and he said everything, everything about her was beautiful. She pressed him as to what was the most beautiful and of course he said her back, that long honey-coloured back that glowed like amber.

'I love her hands,' she had said.

'Her hands,' he had said, puzzled, trying to visualize them, asking if they were long or not long and if Carmen had painted nails and how deep were her cuticles and together and in a spirit of fierce competition they traversed every inch of Carmen's body with Catalina surpassing him in detail about most parts of it and capping each observation with boundless admiration, so much so, that in the end he turned to her and had to admit that he loved her, that he loved her more than anything; Carmen was a dream but she was a reality, a bundle in his arms and he held her and made love to her more ardently than he had ever done. However, she had the last laugh – the next day she left him a bunch of flowers, that she pretended Carmen had sent, and the dolt believed it.

'Have you ever been jealous?' she asked.

'Not like that,' I said, recoiling at the nature of my own jealousy which by contrast was impotent, feeble.

All of a sudden she started to sing. It was in her own tongue. It burst out of her in a great unbridled flow. The whole mountain was filled with it, so that the sheep in their sleep could hear it, as could the distant peaks. At times I thought it was addressed to a man or a woman, certainly a loved one, at other times it meandered like a long Arabic chant. I knew that in it were expressions of pain and longing that cut right down to the bone of the heart, to the bone of night. She did not finish as much as she allowed her voice to trail away, barely audible, then inaudible, yet I felt she was singing a last fragment of it inside her head, a last plea to God, or man or nature or whatever.

'What is it about?'

'It's about an instrument . . . a musical instrument . . . that when pleaded to will bring the bread and the needed woman.'

'Or the needed man,' I said, and saw him flash across the outskirts of my mind, as I had last seen him behind his upstairs window, in a red pullover, a Christmas present I reckoned, as it was Christmas time. I even thought he might look out and be startled to see me skulking there.

'Now it's your turn to sing,' she said.

'Long before Christ, there was an Egyptian sphinx lying on her belly . . . head up . . . bearing two cups towards life . . . a cup of poison and a cup of love.' It was one of those dictums that clung to me, along with another in direct contrast about the special bird having no particular voice, or no particular colour, in short being dun and self-effacing.

'I want to learn it,' she said, 'I want to learn it,' and quietly she confessed that she knew that accretion of poison and love; she bore it in her breast for someone.

Later she took warmed leaves from around the fire and placed them on the bed one by one as if placing patchwork squares or linen roses on a quilt, and as she unpinned my hair and watched the pins fall helter skelter on the floor, she hurrahed. She had wanted to do that for weeks, in fact every time she saw me – my hair was too neat, too groomed, not sauvage enough.

She asked me for a story; one from my own land, an ancient story.

'My father gave me a province of Ireland, the province of Cruachan, which is why I am called "Medb of Cruachan". And as to being asked in marriage,' she said, 'messengers came to me from your own brother, Finn, son of Ross Ruadh, king of Leinster, and I gave him a refusal; and soon after that came messengers from Cairbre Niafer, son of Rossa, king of Teamhair; and from Conchubar, son of Ness, king of Ulster; and after that again from Eochu

Beag, son of Luchta, and I refused them all. For it is not a common marriage portion would have satisfied me, the same as is asked by the other women of Ireland,' she said; 'but it is what I asked as a marriage portion, a man without stinginess, without jealousy, without fear.

'I gave you good wedding gifts,' she said, 'suits of clothing enough for twelve men; a chariot that was worth three times seven serving maids; the width of your face in red gold, the round of your arm in a bracelet of white bronze. You are nothing yourself, but it is in the pay of a woman you are,' she said. 'That is not so,' said Ailell, 'for I am a king's son and I have two brothers that are kings, Finn, king of Leinster, and Cairbre, king of Teamhair, and I would have been king in their places but that they are older than myself. 'You know well,' said Maeve, 'the riches that belong to me are greater than the riches that belong to you.' 'You astonish me,' said Ailell, 'for there is no one in Ireland has a better store of jewels and riches and treasure than myself, and well you know it.'

'Let our goods and our riches be put beside one another, and let a value be put on them,' said Maeve, 'and you will know which of us owns most.' 'I am content to do that,' said Ailell.

With that, orders were given to their people to bring out their goods and to count them, and to put a value on them. They did so, and the first things they brought out were their drinking vessels and all the things belonging to their households, and they were found to be equal. Then their rings were brought out, and their bracelets and chains and brooches, their clothing of crimson and blue and black and green and yellow and saffron and speckled silks and these were found to be equal. Then their great flocks of sheep were driven from the green plains of the open country and were counted, and they were found to be equal; and if there was a ram among Maeve's flocks that was the equal of a serving maid in value, Ailell had one that was as good. And their horses were brought in from the meadows, and their herds of swine out of the woods and the valleys, and were equal one to another. And the last thing that was done was to bring in the herds of cattle from the forest and the wild places of the province, and when they were put beside one another they were found to be equal, but for one thing only.

It happened a bull had been calved in Maeve's herd, and his name was Fionnbanach, the White-Horned. But he would not stop in Maeve's herds, for he did not think it fitting to be under the rule of a woman, and he had gone into Ailell's herds and stopped there; and now he was the best bull in the whole province of Connaught. And when Maeve saw him, and knew he was better than any bull of her own, there was great vexation in her, and it was as bad to her as if she did not own one head of cattle at all. So she called Mac Roth, the herald, to her, and bade him to find out where there was a bull as good as the White-Horned to be got in any province of the provinces of Ireland.

'I myself know that well,' said Mac Roth, 'for there is a bull that is twice as good as himself at the house of Daire, son of Fachtna, in the district of Cuailgne, and that is Don Cuailgne, the Brown Bull of Cuailgne.' 'Rise up then,' said Maeve, 'and make no delay, but go to Daire from me, and ask the loan of that bull for a year.'

'It's beautiful,' she said, and yawned. 'It's very beautiful ... I want to hear it again,' but even as she was talking she fell asleep. Her limbs softened as her bare feet reached to the end of the sagging bed. The candle still guttered and there were spurts of light from the fire, but otherwise the silence and the sense of remoteness were all-pervasive. She breathed lightly and gently and there was in her, in sleep, a fragility that she never allowed in daytime, the artless trustingness of a child. Her mouth was a little open as if, in a dream, she was talking to herself. As I lay beside her I could feel, not our bodies, but our hair touching, ribs of her hair touching mine, charged with inner current. She had left a comb in and the specks of diamanté gleamed in the firelight, like glow worms. I lay there stiffly, quietly confiding to myself that I wanted to hold her, be held by her, but in her sleep, so that our night-selves might reach out, and give each other that thread of sustenance that we craved, the invisible sustenance, not what we sought from men, something other, womanly, primordial. I feared that she might rebuff me, might move away in horror. I feared too that having touched her, something would alter in me. I remembered once coming across a dusky girl, in a café, a café where I had gone to read and to stay as long as possible to fill time. Striking up a conversation I went home later with her, to a huge flat that overlooked Hyde Park and from which one could see the saucered discs of the Post Office Tower and the incline of Parliament Hill. Standing by the window very close to her, I slowly began to undress her, astonished that the lace of her slip was exactly repeated in the lace of her pants and then I laid her down on an extremely white sofa. Everything was white, the leather sofas, the floor rugs, even the upright piano. All of my advances she received without either dismay or flutter. Throughout she remained courteous and did not seem in the least nonplussed by my touch but then within me something occurred, some baulk, some dread, some hesitation and I knew that I could not go through with it. In fact I began to weep. She was kindness itself, stood up, fetched a dressing-gown, escorted me to the bathroom and later gave me several of her cards. She had an apartment in Paris and another in Beirut. Out on the street there was a diminutive man sweeping the gutters, his broom far taller than himself. I threw her cards on his little heap and seeing I was a bit perturbed, he felt obliged to voice the philosophy that no man was worth it.

In her sleep Catalina sometimes stirred and her breath was becoming quicker and more anxious. Dreams. Hosts of them. I will watch over her, I thought. I put my hand across her face, but without touching it. I allowed my hand to hover and thought of the hawk that we had seen that day hovering in the transparent sky. Her eyelids were soft, beautifully soft, like discs of fawn shell; they could have been ornaments. Her cheeks stirred to my near touch and then I waited and it was like seeing the tremors of an animal beneath the ground, a mole maybe. She turned and wakened and there was a kind of quake in the heave of her surprised sigh as she realized where she was and who was next to her. Then I felt the thwack of her arms around me and the clasp of her hands, and I stretched out and cleaved to her, through her opening to life; arms, limbs, torsos, joined as if in an androgynous sculpture, the bloods going up and down merrily, two bloods, like mercury in a heated thermometer, even the cheeks letting go all of their scream and all their grumble and their thousand unspent kisses; tenderness, rabidness; hunger, back, back in time to that wandering milky watery bliss, infinitely safe like wine inside a skin or sap inside a tree, floating, afloat; boundaries burst, bursting, the mind as much as the body borne along, to this other landscape, that was familiar yet unfamiliar, like entering a picture, or a fresco, slipping through a wall of flesh, eclipsed, inside the womb of the world, and throughout it all her words, faint, sweet as vapour.

In the morning she fetched two bottles of water and without even asking she poured one over each of us so that it streamed down on to our faces, our bodies, a baptism at once reckless and cleansing. She had brought leaves as well and she pressed them all over me like poultices or face flannels.

It was a little thing and I don't know why it occurred to me but suddenly I was telling her. I had been in Madrid a long time before, twenty years before, and had gone to a bullfight, it being the season. It was my first bullfight and I was taken by some very smart people. From time to time I would say something, something innocuous or ridiculous, just to let them know that I was there. Afterwards as they all gloated and discussed moves and the various passes, I agreed, like a sheep, except that I was bleeding, bleeding from the spectacle. I bled for the entire week, in sympathy, with either the bulls or the horses or the young picadors or the strutting daring matadors, or the whole ritual which by its spectacle, its terror and its gore brought to my mind too vividly Christ's bleeding wounds and the women I knew, including myself, as if Christ was woman and woman was Christ in the bloodied ventricles of herself. Man in woman and woman in man. The impossible. And during that week, one of those nights when we ate very late and drank jugs and jugs of wine and then peppermint frappés, a woman in our party, an Eastern woman with black brilliantined hair and an amber choker, decided to read the coffee cups, and when it came to my turn, when she read mine, her face flinched as she turned to my friend and said, 'She hasn't done it right, she's not doing it right,' and like a fool I reached for my cup thinking I had not shaken the dregs of coffee enough or allowed the grains to settle in the right way. But it was too late, what she was telling me was, that I drank and ate and lived and perceived life the wrong way. She looked at me with scorn and I knew, as I had always feared, that I was only scraping through and that death would be my only redemption.

'No tinguis por...' Catalina said.

'What is that?'

'Don't be afraid,' she said, then she kissed me and the kiss was a seal. Her face was beautiful and not beautiful, it was a little swarthy and wet from the baptism. Our night was not something to fear either, but to carry within us, not as a memory of debauch, but a constant, like one of those streams or rills that one hears when walking along a country road, but that one does not see, simply knows it to be there.

Outside the world was enveloped in mist, the topmost points of the mountain like grey carbuncles. The trees and the bushes were baggy, caught in this mist and a herd of blue-black goats that ran in front of us were like phantoms. She ran on ahead, making sure that this time we would not miss our bus. She was brisk, probably already in her mind tackling the day's duties while I wondered if I should get a chance to see her again. As if she read my thoughts she broke off a huge spray of lilac up at the bus stop.

'Show them that in London,' she said, both a farewell and a reprimand for resuming my city existence.

Seventeen

I was happy to be going home, full of that little flutter that the prospect of a journey brings. I saw corners of England that I might glimpse from a train: a field of corn, bronzed; black and white cows with enormous pink udders wading in a stream, the crows rising, settling, then rerising like bits of black gauze in the sky, taking flight from a single tractor that seemed as lonely as a spaceship. I had left her a note and a little money to put towards buying a scooter. I had left it with the nunnish girl, the girl with the moustache, who because I was leaving had capitulated somewhat, even said, 'We will miss you . . . it is our hope that you will return.'

That evening and for the second time in my long stay I ate in the big dining room. It was very solemn eating alone like that, baroque music drifting from the gallery, big stout beeswax candles, church candles, their flames veering this way and that, trying to break from the blue interiors that formed webs around the wicks. The wine glasses were so wide and deep, they were like fingerbowls, and drinking from them I felt pampered, giddy. Afterwards I took an amaretto and sat in the garden. The lights along the wall were covered with pink roof tiles which transmitted a shower of radiance, the lining a frailer pink, not like stone at all, but like flesh, and something about these colours and these exquisite drained tints reminded me of her and of him, as if love itself was a beautiful warm glow, a lamp inside of one. It was late when I left the garden and as I came through the hotel I lingered for a moment in the salon. The photographer from Cologne, Charlotte, Iris, they whisked through my mind like living ghosts, people I would probably never see again.

At dawn someone burst into my room. I thought perhaps that I had overslept and that it was the young boy come with my last luxurious breakfast. Hurriedly I reached for a dressing-gown, or a shawl, only to hear a girl screaming at me, calling me 'Puta . . . Puta', 'Whore . . . Whore'. I thought at first that it must be the putty-faced woman who had accosted me on the way down from the church but soon, as I clicked on the light, I saw that it was Rosario, Catalina's sister, wild, demented, her hair uncombed and her eyes full of raging tears. I had ruined her family, I had destroyed their honour. Honour was the word she spouted most as she repeated the story again and again. They had been asleep, her father had got up early to go out and smoke his pipe and had seen it. It. It. It. 'Lesbos' had been painted on their wall for all to see. I saw it in terrifying and graphic reality. It was black, as she said, and bold, as she said, and it would not wash out, or scratch out and anyhow it was too late. Everyone had seen it, her mother, her aunt, neighbouring women, all aghast at what they saw. Aghast and ashamed. Was Catalina capable of such a thing, such violation. Their own bodies no doubt partook of her shame and curdled in horror. I imagined them swarming into the hotel and stoning me.

'Do you see what you have done?' she kept saying. She described each second of it, her father getting up, going out, seeing some young boys up a tree and thinking they had come to steal the apricots, then suddenly seeing it.

'Lesbos Lesbos Lesbos!' she shrieked, as if I had not already heard, then she described his going back into the house, wakening them, dragging Catalina from her bed, her having to fight him with her bare arms, still half asleep, shouting, 'What? What?' because of course she did not know.

'We're ruined . . . ruined!' she kept saying. Each time I tried to reason with her she would counter with another accusation. She had seen it coming for weeks. Her father had seen it too, her mother being too busy and too overworked to see anything. I had deliberately destroyed their good name. She could have foretold it. They were one of the oldest families in the parish and I had usurped their honour in one swoop. Her command of English was great and I remembered that Catalina had told me that she had worked in London for six months but had had to be brought back because of her homesickness. They were decent people, as she said, frugal, they worked the land, she allowed herself one packet of cigarettes per week; yet whenever they mixed with strangers it led to trouble and disaster. Why the presents to Catalina? Why the lunches and dinners? Why go to the mountain, why insist on staying all night? Why? Why? The shame was killing her. Her mother, she said, had fallen down in a faint. Her mother who not only worked the farm and the house but took in washing, so as to save for the little boy's education.

'How is Catalina?' I said.

'How is she!' she shrieked. I ought to know that she was black and blue, that she had gone to her bedroom and locked the door and most likely she would never come out. Her father had beaten her savagely, in front of the neighbours, and but for her grandmother he might have killed her.

'It's all lies,' I said.

'Then prove it,' she said. 'Prove it,' and she almost struck me.

'I'll go to the priest,' I said, feeling myself hauled right back to that state of childhood trying to brazen out some terrible confrontation with adults, while quaking within.

'You had better go . . .' she said. 'You had better . . .'

'Leave me,' I said with as much authority as I could muster, and even as she was leaving I had my hand on the dial to ask the girl at the desk to change my reservation on the aeroplane.

Ripped-off petals of geraniums lay all along the ground in pools, looking like those vivid scarlet hearts painted on to Valentine cards. The outdoor trestle table made of driftwood was drenched but in places the sun had just begun to suck the moisture from it so that its surface was dappled like a lake and its unshaven edges jutted like cropped fur. Young vines on the terrace were an artificial green, as if they had been treated to one of those essences with which people dye cakes or icing; their delicate stalks curling upwards, threading their way flawlessly through a lattice, to the light.

I had waited until a reasonable hour to call on D'Arcy, in his mountain abode, only to find him in a wild agitation, kicking oatmeal all over the floor and screaming obscenities. Each time he kicked, he coupled the obscenity with a world leader, a dynastic figure who was personally responsible for this most recent wallop of excruciating fate.

'What's for breakfast – Bacon is off, fuck the Queen.

'What's for brunch – Eggs Benedict is off, fuck Reagan.

'What's for tea – muffins is off, fuck Thatcher.

'Croissant, brioche and baguettes is off – fuck Mitterand, De Gaulle, the little Corporal and the syphilitic Louis.

'Spuds is off – fuck Fianna Fáil and fuck Fine Gael.'

He ceased from his barrage to acknowledge my arrival. The kitchen, or what passed for a kitchen, was in chaos, tins of paint and paintings everywhere, including the two Van Goghs facing each other, with what seemed to be galling contempt. He said that I might at least have warned him, apprised him of this unprecedented visit, might have sent a calling card, a bush telegram, anything. Yes, he was in a foul humour, and he would like to say, and he would like posterity to note, that he had been revolving around the fucking universe on his arse and his axis for fifty-seven years and that he had had enough ... Basta, Basta, Basta.

The reason for this excess of rage and for oatmeal scattered everywhere was that he was being evicted, having already lost his studio in the town. This little casita which he had inhabited for two years, was an annex of a big house higher up and he had just received a letter from the piss-arse absentee owner that all was sold to a fucking foreigner, Hitler's valet's illegitimate grandson or a Zimbabwe arms dealer no doubt. He was used to spartan living as he so gloatingly said, but he was not used to being told to scarper at a moment's notice, and worse he would have to leave his garden, his pride, his paradise, where he had planted marrows, corn salad, arugula; where he had spent wholesome hours treating that soil to care and fondnesses that he had never treated a woman to.

'Where to fucking go?' he asked as he vowed to dig up every little seedling, every bean pod, every sprout that would have been a potato or a flourish of potatoes; he would dig them up and give them to the animals as swill. He asked Christ, Judas, Simon Zealot and sundry martyrs why he was cursed so, why like Branwell Brontë did the muse once attend, then subsequently forsake him. He too was a child prodigy and could write in two languages with either hand and, moreover, could read Walter Pater, at six or seven, could say Mass in Latin.

'Every day, or every other day, I stagger up to that fucking graveyard and I speak to the dead ... any old dead, and I say, "Help D'Arcy to turn over a new leaf ... no more drink, no more debauch ... no more pipe dreams ... let D'Arcy drink of the milk of human kindness instead of this goddamn putrid whey ... let D'Arcy's pulse beat with a merry rhythm," and does it happen ... No ... No ... No ... it's Eviction, Bankruptcy, Ridicule!' and he hit his head savagely against the stone of the unplastered wall.

I thought of leaving but I had only to remember Rosario's screams and hisses to me 'to do something'. I blurted it out.

'Down McQuarie Street were ye?' he said, adding that he had always thought that I was still snooping about for a young Lochinvar or a not-so-young Lochinvar, a Byronic bastard.

'Did ye use a catheter?' he asked gleefully, his temper leavening as he rose to the challenge. He wished to know the colour of the graffiti, the approximate size, if it had been done by a hack or in a legible hand, was bold or *trompe l'oeil*.

'I haven't seen it ... I've only been told about it.' He doubled over, laughing, said it would titillate the town for a week, bars would be full, he D'Arcy would get free drink, might even get to shack up somewhere with someone and as he enthused the colour came back into his cheeks and the blue galvanized eyes grew moist with tears of laughter.

'I love it . . . I love it!' he said and he ran around the room, offering me now sodden biscuits from a packet, proffering an empty beer bottle, simulating largesse; then suddenly from under a knitted tea cosy he pulled a little mouth organ and began to play with fervour. He sang a line of the song between each bar of melody:

> '. . . On Boulavogue, as the sun was setting . . .
> O'er in the bright May meadows of Shalemiler
> A rebel hand got the heather blazing . . .'

He had a solution that was Einsteinian, Archimedian . . . mind-shattering, would boggle the biddies and the bastards, keep them guessing and cogitating until Michaelmas.

'What is it?'

'Suffice to say that it involves the decorative arts . . . so now leave me to reconnoitre, and then to execute it and by this time tomorrow your name will be cleared . . . Up the Queen, up Reagan, up Thatcher and up Fianna Fáil, Fine Gael! . . . forget the Frogs . . .'

He played very fast then, signalling me out the way a gypsy disposes of an admiring crowd in a restaurant. He wanted no remuneration until the deed was done and then I could see that he was made a Chevalier or given the Legion of Honour but please no OBE or CBE which sounded like a kidney complaint. Outside the sun was blazing, and seeing it flow back into everything was like watching blood being transfused back into a corpse. The air was suffused with light, the earth soaked with it, as were the plants, the trees, the stones, the vegetation, even the little bed of parsley that he proudly pointed to.

'You came to the right man,' he said and assured me that the task ahead would give him immense satisfaction. As an

afterthought he added that it might be a good idea if I were
to call on the ecumenical-minded priest.

'You are a very villain else,' he said and warned that I give
him a handsome sum, a nugget. However he thought it most
fitting and most laudable that I had come first to David
Anthony Ignatius Donne, the unfrocked priest who might
now be a missioner in clink or a paunchy curate in Ballinasloe.
He ruminated about his long years in the seminary, a vocation
that he wrestled with, and how the Fathers tried to keep him
against his will except that he bested them, got the runs
at all hours, fouling their quarters, giving their incensed
corridors a whiff of bog.

'You never told me,' I said.

'Must I . . .' he quoted, 'Must I ravel out my weav'd up
follies.' Like all lonely people but particularly those who
revile their loneliness, he would not let me go, but sent
snippets, bulletins along the terrace, finding story after story
to regale me with.

Later, walking along, I was douched with water and when
I looked up I saw that my assailants were two youths, who
sniggered.

'They're only youngsters,' I said but already I had begun
to walk very fast and my feet in their canvas shoes seemed
to traverse the rubble of the path without actually touching
it.

The priest's house adjoined the church but I waited until
the church door was barred for the night and the faithful had
gone home. His door was opened, not as I had expected by
a housekeeper, but by a very young boy on roller-skates.
Down the length of the long dark hallway I could see into a
room, where there was a party in progress, with other young
boys whizzing around on roller-skates. One of them had put
a hand over the priest's eyes to stop his seeing something on
television. On the screen, in a black and white film, a couple
were kissing, the woman bent back like a reed. Wanda's son
was beating egg whites with a fork. He said my name, to
show the others that he knew me. The priest was not nearly
so cordial. He was in white trousers and red turtle-neck

sweater and finding me in the room came as a jolt to him. He composed himself as much as he could by pulling his sweater down over his protruding stomach. He was holding a currant biscuit which he endeavoured to disguise, by curling his fingers around it. No longer young, it was obvious that his appearance mattered greatly to him. He wore a brunette toupee that was lighter and finer than his own hair, and not being ample enough for his large head, it looked more like a skullcap. He rose and put his hand out, signalling me to return to the hallway, refusing to receive me in his kitchen.

The audience was in a very dark and sombre room filled with heavy pieces of brown furniture. In a toneless voice he greeted me, asked in halting English what he could do for me. I replied in his language, having learnt the phrase over and over again. I had come to ask to have a Mass said, to have it announced, so that the whole village would know. I had the money ready. He took it almost daintily, as a fat man might take a sugar cube from a tongs. He made some attempt at a smile but it was more like folds over his bucolic features. For something to say I admired the room and its sombre contents. He said, yes, that his old chest and his mirrors were very dear to him and that of course they did not fade as a woman fades, even the prettiest woman. Suddenly he asked if I wanted him to hear my confession and as I was taken by surprise I said yes. He opened a drawer and pulled out a purple stole which he donned over his turtle-neck sweater. I knelt and while I was muttering generalizations, two of the little cupids popped their heads through the door, and the absurd spectacle of me kneeling and him presiding over me sent them rushing to the kitchen, squealing and laughing, to tell the others. He became quite theatrical as he spouted the absolution and afterwards as he saw me out he corrected me on one matter of history, said that although there was a large statue of Saint Sebastian in the church, he was not their patron saint, their patron saint was John the Baptist.

'No arrows,' he said. And I was not sure whether that was

offered as some sort of consolation or a reward for the lavish offering I had given him. I imagined him putting it into one of the big brown chests, then hurrying back to the friskiness of the kitchen, where the egg whites would have been whisked to a magic foam.

Eighteen

It was mid-morning and the lorries were arriving from the town bringing crates of beer and wooden boxes of fish laced with thin icicles. The village buzzed with it. Many laughed, but those on whose walls it appeared were incensed. The postmistress, flushed and fuming, paced with a coat over her nightgown and a look of bloated indignation on her sallow face. It was as if she might explode, or a glut of violence might come bursting out. She would stand and point to it, the blond stone of her harmless house on which the black obscenity had been scrawled: LESBOS. LESBOS. It had been perfectly and legibly sprayed, for all to see. D'Arcy had done a superlative job. At times she shouted, then at other times strode back and forth talking to herself, mulling vengeance, calling to one of the other women to help her, to come to her aid, in this brazen heathen time. One of the maids from my hotel reported that it was on two other walls and was rumoured to be on the main wall before one arrived in the town, the wall that had 'Welcome' on it. D'Arcy had not been sparing. The offending words, perfectly sprayed, graced the wall of the post office, a private house, the mayor's garden wall, and as this girl said, the gateway to the town. D'Arcy himself was nowhere to be seen but I reckoned that he would appear by lunch, suave, shaven, chuffed at the brilliance of his scheme, and that as he sat down to eat with me, or stood at one of the bars to quaff, he could discuss it with the others, and debate as to whether it was of Roman or Byzantine influence. The little cupids that I had seen at the priest's house sought bribes so they could ride out of town and count how many other walls it appeared on.

At lunch-time I went to the restaurant owned by the two sisters and felt a little triumphant as I entered. The ladies welcomed me with a feigned cordiality but at least they did not bar the way. I ordered a bottle of the local wine, and the local soup which was clogged with bread, vegetables and specks of brown so simmered that they were either mushrooms or shreds of rabbit meat.

'Gusta . . . gusta,' one of them said as I looked at my soup, reluctant to eat, waiting, hoping that D'Arcy would come, my eye on the stairway that shelved directly up from the street. On the other side of the restaurant was a bar, where there was laughing and roistering, no doubt the customers, the foreigners that is, using the excitement of the morning to drink a little more.

Wanda came up the stairs and ran to my table, excited. Had I heard? She was opening a new boutique, in no time she would be flying to major cities to buy fashions and accessories.

At first she would just stock local stuff, embroidered blouses and knitwear, but in time she would have designer clothes, she would buy from the small designers, she would travel, she would go all over the world . . . she would call her boutique 'Zara'.

Hearing that I was leaving she said it was a pity that we had not become friends, particularly as she was the one to have met me that first morning. The puppy that her son had kept was bigger now and even in heat and would probably soon be propositioned by her father or her grandfather.

'Talk of vice,' she said, and declared the place to be a Peyton Place under the sheets.

She, like everyone, had seen the postmistress's fulminations, and laughed as she recalled that at the church fair the previous Christmas the postmistress had bought the only baby-doll nightie and matching knicks.

'To burn them?' I said.

'Maybe not,' she said with a half smile, 'maybe she's keeping them in her bottom drawer, just in case.'

'How's your son?' I said.

'An angel,' she said. 'I went in last night to give him a little peck and he had a cabbage leaf on his pillow to catch the ladybirds . . .' As she said it her features dissolved into a radiant smile.

'I saw him at the priest's house.'

'Oh yes . . . they go up there and watch TV and make whoopee,' she said. Then she confessed that she had been a little hurt that she had not seen much of me, that I had given my affections elsewhere. I imagined she was referring to Catalina and that she was intrigued by the rumour, and would have loved to pry.

'I'll come back,' I said, on an impulse. I even asked her to keep her eyes out for a little place for me, a holding with a terrace and a small orchard. The mention of it brought tears to her eyes. It was as if in this promise, rashly given, I had made a bond with her. She would keep her eyes open, she knew all the properties; people moving in, people moving out, she knew where to find a bargain, way off in the hills, moreover she knew auctions, markets, flea markets, everything, we could furnish it for a song. Then a youngster came in to tell her that the water-man was at her house waiting to be paid; and she ran out, imploring me to come back before the end of the summer.

Not long after, a young man came in, dressed in black, black sweater and worn black velveteen pants. One of the sisters bowed to him but it was a formal bow, not a greeting. Under his beard his face was very pale and there was something pent-up about him. Over his shoulders he wore a black overcoat which he allowed to drop off, at the same moment as he stood by the sideboard and helped himself to some red wine. His hair was so shaven that he looked like an embryo; his eyes vortexes of hurt and rage. No one spoke to him although it was clear that they knew him, as there was the occasional nod in his direction. He sat alone at a long table and ate ravenously. He was cosmopolitan and had a little tattoo on his wrist, it was an eye, a blue eye with thick indigo lashes. I thought perhaps that he might be an actor with a troupe of travelling players, or that he made jewellery or ceramics which he had come to sell. At moments he would turn around as if he knew that I was watching him, as if to challenge me, and his stare was at once insolent and begging. He was proud of the way he allowed his body to swivel and when he waved a hand to one of the sisters to bring him another glass of wine, he gave the impression of being a ventriloquist, as if something might drop from his sleeve. When he heard that the coffee machine was broken he looked at her with such disdain and then laughed riotously and said, 'La machina kaput,' he expected us to laugh with him, but no one did. She offered him instant coffee which he declined. Then he thought for a moment as if lost in some reverie, stood up and looked around, sneeringly as if he was looking at a bunch of sheep not worthy of his slaughter. He slipped the coat over his shoulders capewise and went down the stairs slowly, like an actor going on stage.

'Who is he?' I asked one of the sisters.

'He come here ... sometime ... he travel,' she said.

'Is he a gypsy?' I said and she smiled at my simple notion of supposing anyone eccentric to be a gypsy.

'He not gypsy, he heself,' she said but I knew that she feared him and also that he had not paid his bill.

D'Arcy did not appear and eventually I left, saying goodbye somewhat ceremoniously to the sisters and the remaining guests. Outside the street was so empty, it might have just been sacked, it had that desertedness of streets in westerns just before the fatal shoot-out. The shops were closed for the siesta and even the big brown unglazed pots seemed to have surrendered to sleep. I would sleep too, in my beautiful little room that had changed from being a cell to a haven with its flowers and its candles and its emanations of her. I went up the hill to see the sea, to have a last look at it. It was a sheer blue, with wavelets, like gulls' wings tilting upwards to form an unending blue frill and still soft green patches of cloudlike water underneath the rock with the hole in it. I stood there wondering if I would come back, wondering what it was that sent me to this place, rather than any other believing, knowing that it was her. The mountains seemed nearer too, more amenable, as if one could reach out and touch them. Somewhere up there was the spot where I had lain with her, and I thought, even after we are dead places carry emanations of us.

A young boy of about ten or eleven came up behind me on a scooter to deliver a message and hand me a bunch of dried flowers. She wished to see me after dark at the little casita . . . Ca'an Serra.

'Why has she not written?' I asked.

'She is afraid,' he said very earnestly, and then added, 'I am her cousin,' as if in that simple remark there resided every guarantee of sincerity. Then he was gone as quickly and as stealthily as he arrived and soon I saw his bicycle down on the track that led to the sea, bouncing and bounding like a surfer. It had to be she. Who else would be sending me dried flowers, flowers such as we had seen on the mountain. But even if it were not she I would have to go for her sake.

The afternoon dragged on. I repacked various glass ornaments, put them into nightgowns and sweaters to keep them from breaking. Anything to make time pass. At four I ordered tea and the rich fruit cake that I had so often and so wilfully declined. Long before it arrived I was feasting on the big green shreds of candied peel and the moist glacé cherries. They rang from reception to ask what kind of tea I wanted and later they rang to ask if I would be settling my account by cheque or by bankers' card. Both times I jumped. Yet I could not confide in anyone, the whole thing having become so clandestine. Foolishly I thought of writing to my sons, saying the trenchant things that I had refrained from, but this too I thought to be a bit extreme. I knew that in an office in Lincoln's Inn Fields was the will I had made, and immediately chided myself for being so superstitious, so timorous.

At sundown I set out, reckoning that it would be dark by

the time I arrived. The mountains were tapestries now, dun-
gold and russet. I did not take the donkey track but went
along the main road where I met a few people, the couple
who owned an art gallery and from whom I had bought the
glass ornaments, an excitable visitor in a dark suit with a soft
brown hat carrying an open bottle of wine and talking to
himself. I passed various gateways, some shut for the night,
others open with several cars in the drive. As I walked it
grew dark and once I got on to the terraces, I felt less
sanguine. To calm myself I tried to imagine the waves coming
in on the broken chain of seashore, coming in slowly, softly,
then breaking into shreds, like guipure lace, then receding
to allow for the next swoop. As I climbed higher I got
out my little torch and would look in the other direction,
expecting to see hers, which for economy's sake she would
keep flicking on and off.

The door was not locked, and as I pushed it in, I heard a
thud and thought perhaps that my worst suspicions were
founded. By the light of the torch I saw that it was the cat
which had jumped from the chair to the door and which
miaowed with hunger. In all the dramas, the goats had probably not been milked. Sidling back on to a chair it decided
to ignore me. As I shone the torch about the room something
in me petrified. The place was untidy, seeds and bulbs all
over the table and a little hand plough in the centre of the
floor. I felt that somehow she would have got there ahead of
me to move these things. In one corner there was a baby's
high-chair with beads that stretched across it. I touched
them, allowing them to clonk back and forth on a piece of
plastic cord. Occasionally I went outside to see if there was
any sign of her. The young moon was a mould of silver with
a greenish hue to it and not a single person moved on any of
the terraces either above or below. She was perhaps biding
her time. She had to come. I could feel her presence, her
voice, her warmth. Inside the house I thought of going into
the other room but suddenly conceived this dread that there
was someone in there waiting for me, waiting for us. I talked
to myself, talked reams to banish these fears. It may have

been a quarter of an hour or it may have been less, but suddenly I heard a roar followed by a splutter of roars, so awful, it was as if a herd of swine was being slaughtered again and again. It could have been a man or a woman, the gender being impossible to tell because of the pitch and the delirium of it. The cat jumped, leapt through the air, crazed like a monkey and clawed at the door to get out. There was a supernatural energy to its movements and as I pulled the door open I was sure it flew. The roar had subsided to a murmur, more like a prayer or a series of prayers, and I thought maybe it meant some sort of procession and that the locals had come together to pray for their crops. I ran to the terrace higher up, the one that I thought would bring me by a more direct route to them. Instead it led me to an incline where there was a sheep dip, which I scrambled over, hoping to find a path beyond. Then the torch gave out. Plunged now in darkness except for the light from the moon I ran hither and thither, seeing the same things, paths, trees, the sheep dip, heaps of stones, again and again retracing my steps so that in the end I had to hang my scarf on a tree to serve as a landmark. I could hear the sounds of cars coming and going, car doors being banged and I knew that there had been some accident.

Eventually as I neared the main road I heard the bells, two bells in steady and alternating sequence, one deep and pounding, the other lighter in tone, both with a sense of portent. I knew it, a second before I could have known it, that it boded death, yet I hesitated before running to ask.

'Campana grave ... campana aquida,' the voices said. Voices talking rapidly but in a hush, talking and blessing themselves, then waiting for the next peal.

'He do by knife,' a woman said, and shook her head at such barbaric rites.

'Who is it?' I asked one of the younger girls.

'Pimpinella...' she said, and for a moment I believed it was a stranger.

'Catalina Espert ... the daughter of Tomás and Conchita

Espert,' an older woman added and then began to ream off
the names of grandparents and great-grandparents from both
scions of the family. The young girl cried openly, wildly.
They were friends, she and Catalina, they had been at school
together, acted in plays together. Catastrophe strikes the
body first, long before it reaches the brain. I felt as if being
gouged.

'He kill her at last,' a younger woman said.

'Who killed her?' I asked, thinking that maybe it was her
father, still livid from the disgrace over the graffiti.

'Her husband ... Juan,' the young girl said and turned
away.

The head waiter was coming down the street, his jacket
over his shoulder, his gait nonchalant and I ran to him as if
he could avert it.

'Her husband ... he cut her throat,' he said calmly.

'Husband?' I said.

'Enfante-Juan ... she maybe never told you ... She keep
it a secret even from most of us in the hotel ... but I know
... we close our doors to him way back.'

'Who was he?'

'A punk,' he said, 'from the very south ... hot blood ...
he try to kill a waiter in the hotel over nathing ... he think
the waiter flirt with har.'

'So the child was theirs too?'

'Yes ... they go to court over him two times, they have
blood testing,' he said, his dry words in contrast with the
bedlam.

Not long before, Juan had been brought to the police
station, a blanket over his head crying out that he loved her,
that he wanted to die with her.

I knew he must be the man I had seen in the restaurant
and I believed now that it was him and not her who had sent
the message by the little boy and that the little boy must have
panicked at the last minute and told her. She had gone out
to meet him, to meet the fate that was meant for me. I ran
from one place to another as if running could undo it. What
did I know of death – nothing. What did I know of life –

nothing. The bar was empty and so was Wanda's house. Cats were on the table gorging on a bowl of chocolate mix. They looked grotesque. Everywhere people were talking, hurrying, children being comforted as they believed that they too were about to be murdered. I caught up with the women that had started down the donkey track, linked to keep each other from falling or fainting. Each new disclosure killed her afresh so that by the time we got to the bridge she had died a thousand times.

'He donta care ... he donta look for a way to hide har ... he carry har ... he drink har blood ... he say I lave har ... he carry har to har mother's house,' a woman said to me. She was the woman who coiffed my hair each week and who was normally a model of reserve, sweeping the shop floor or stringing beans, as I sweltered under the wobbling drier, but now charged, unfettered. She and her aunt laid out the corpse, all in a short space, because mourners started to arrive once they heard the news. They were the last to carry on the tradition. She spoke of their task with a mixture of pride and revulsion. She had had to run home to change. The blood was everywhere, even under her nails she said, holding her hands out. Still they had done a good job, they had made her look beatific ... 'beata, beata.' She longed to say more, to wallow in it.

Where the road forked near a tavern there were a few men backing out of a house carrying an invalid.

'Enferma – Enferma,' the woman whispered. Under the hazed shower of light from the street lamp I saw a man's face, thin, wizened, mouth agape. They were taking him to the house to taste death. Death for one meant death for all. Their sorrow bound them together.

'La voz de Díos ... La voz de Díos,' they said as he stared up at them. Catalina had been a friend to him, she bathed his sores sometimes when his married daughter could not come.

As we neared the house I saw Charlotte at the gate smoking. She looked very tall and incongruous in her jeans, her face blurred. It was she who had found them, on the way to the village to sell her Walkman. She ran and clung to me like a long-lost friend. She was shaking, stammering, repeating the events as she had repeated them to the family, to the police, to the priest, to the coroner, to endless neighbours and now to me, how she had met him, how he had a wild excited look in his eyes, how he had told her to get out of his way and how she had hurried off in fear. Soon after he met Catalina and she had heard their raised voices and their first bitter exchanges and she ran faster, not wishing to overhear. When she heard the roar, Catalina's roar, she knew what it was, what it meant and again she relived the moments herself; pausing in disbelief, in horror, then running, tripping over the knife that he had dropped, picking it up, its feel warm and wet, like bloodied flesh. Here, she breaks down completely, recounting the ghastly minutes that followed, his trying to give Catalina the kiss of life, her having to run on ahead, finding the mother in the yard rounding up geese, the mother refusing to believe it, then having to believe it once she beheld the gruesome tableau, his blood-smeared face, his voice crying to his Maker. She clutched me then, said she had heard some of the young men talking, they intended to take me for a drive, their brother Juan would have his honour restored. He had been drinking with them all afternoon down at the sea and undoubtedly they had filled his head with tales. He had had a rendezvous with me.

'They can't do anything to me,' I said.

'They can ... on a night like this they can do anything,' she said. Nothing would deter me. My fear had been replaced by stunned horror and a scalding shame. Had I never come to this place, had I never met her she might now be sitting down to her supper or washing her hair and for the cruellest of seconds I saw her alive as on that first morning, full of arch gaiety, throwing flowers about like wet fish.

There was a crowd in the garden, mostly men, talking and drinking, but in the dark I could not distinguish them. I saw D'Arcy, his back turned, standing over the invalid, holding a jug of wine. From the room, came the prayers and the oration – 'Decanza Eterna ... Lux Perpetua ...' 'Eternal Rest

... Perpetual Light...' As I went through the door her sister
rose to bar the way, followed by three others, all in black.
Her mother was closest to the bed, the women standing over
her weeping, like extras in one of the Stations of the Cross.
I could not see Catalina's face, only the very white covers
that reached to her chin like wadding. Where was her soul
now? I recalled those books that I had read, depicting that
long journey after death, sphere after sphere before reaching
the final destination. Death took root in me then, as for so
many years love had, and to such excruciating purpose,
but who in their right minds would not exchange love for
death?

'Get out of here ... get out of here,' her sister screamed,
the others repeating it exactly as they pushed me out. It was
what the men in the garden had been waiting for, this cue
from the women, this call for revenge. They gathered round
me, heated, obstreperous. There were about ten of them,
some recognizing me and telling the others who I was, the
whore, the foreign whore. Hatreds that they did not even
know of, glistened on their faces, hatreds fuelled by their
drunken spunk. One of them tapped my chest, quick insolent
taps as if it were a drum-skin or a table-top. They made no
secret of their wishes, jerked their heads and said, 'Vamos,
Vamos' – 'let us go.'

In jest one of them lifted my hair, gave a lewd sniff and
then pulled me by it to the gate. I saw a van and saw us go
towards it. A young man got in and turned on the headlights
and in the swoosh of light I saw their legs and their feet in
high-heeled leather boots, then their faces, some chalky,
others with sideburns and moustaches. My assassins.

D'Arcy came rushing towards us, his drink in his hand.
He spoke to the ringleader, said his name, 'Pablo ... Pablo,'
while one of the others pushed me into the van, next to
the lascivious young driver. They formed a huddle around
D'Arcy, several of them talking and shouting. They seemed
to disagree on what they had to say because some would push
others aside and go close to him to air their version. Then
one of them shook hands with him. He must have said

something mocking or insulting because all of a sudden things escalated. Pablo, grabbing D'Arcy's glass, smashed it on the mudguard, to use the splinters as weapons. I saw D'Arcy open his shirt, challenging them, goading them and soon he was on the ground as they converged on him. Charlotte ran up the pathway, dragging Catalina's mother who looked as if she herself had been called from the dead. She was like one of those trees felled in a storm, its roots naked, obscene, gaping helplessly back at life. She moved among them shouting and they drew back, suddenly compliant, ashamed. Pablo put his folded hands towards her in a gesture of clemency and then he spoke to her rapidly, obviously trying to persuade her to let the men settle the vendetta themselves. At the same moment the driver started the engine and accelerated and I knew with certainty that he was going to ride over D'Arcy, crush him to death. With one hand I pulled at the handbrake and with the other grabbed the steering wheel and we tugged and wrestled over it, as might two people in a bumper-car at a funfair. It careered all over the road, then lurched to one side and dropped like a wounded beast.

D'Arcy was speaking to the mother and I went towards them to say something though I did not know what. The look she gave me was terrifying. It was a cold pitiless look that said, 'You may not have killed my daughter but you were the precursor of it, the Bad Shepherd.' I put my hand out and she stared at it as if it was a leper's, then she turned and said something to Charlotte. It might have been a stone oracle that spoke, so stilted was her voice.

'She's broken . . . she's completely broken,' D'Arcy said.

'I have to speak to her,' I said.

'Speak. Bull,' he said with a savage glare as if I should know that we are each alone with our crime, unable to bear it, unable to give it away. Then, less harshly, he proposed that we make ourselves scarce. Yes, he was saying as he put an arm around me, yes, it had all begun so blithely that Easter morning and it had come to this. As we walked I heard the gate close with a clang, like a cemetery gate when the mourners have gone. I was too mortified to turn round to wave to Charlotte.

'Upon my vesture they have cast lots,' he said, making light of his wounds and joking about his tattered shirt. Scuts they were, hardly even knew Juan whom they so proudly defended. Nor was it any use accusing myself, it happened, it was on the cards from the very first day he and Catalina met; enfante Juan, led by a polar star, spouting Nietzsche – 'the City reeks of the slaughterhouse ... I am joyful in my winter sorrow,' and so forth, elopement, bambalino, hostilities, the old story.

'It had to be,' he said with a kind of awful compassion, then he reeled towards the low wall of the tavern, calling his friend, 'Kevin ... Kev.' He said that the sooner I scooted the better, as passions might run amok again, indeed would, once the hearse came.

'Calla Aparte ... Parting of the Ways,' he said. In a way it was the worst moment of all, the banishment.

Going down the road a figure appeared out of the darkness. I thought it was one of the young men but turned to see a little woman, a wisp of a thing. I knew it was the grandmother. She was wearing a threadbare black coat which flapped on her as though on a hat-stand. She handed me something in a scarf. It felt warm. I thought it was a dead bird or entrails, a curse, but as she undid the knot I saw Catalina's hair, so vibrant, so alive, it was as if her face still adhered to it. Under the moon it glistened, black for the most part but red where it was matted with blood. She put her lips to it.

'Muy precioso ... muy precioso,' she said, her voice cracked and choking. But it was with a kind of ecstasy that she gave it to me. Take it, she was saying, for to love one must learn to part with everything. Then she was gone, hobbling like an unfledged bird or a creature on stilts.

The road grew dark and bright at one and the same instant and for the last time I set out for home.